SONS, LOVERS, ETCETERA

SONS, LOVERS, ETCETERA

Vida Adamoli

Copyright © 1997 Vida Adamoli

The right of Vida Adamoli to be identified as the Author of the Work has been asserted by her in accordance with the Copyright, Designs and Patents Act 1988.

First published in 1997
by HEADLINE BOOK PUBLISHING

A HEADLINE REVIEW hardback

10 9 8 7 6 5 4 3 2 1

All rights reserved. No part of this publication may be reproduced, stored in a retrieval system, or transmitted, in any form or by any means without the prior written permission of the publisher, nor be otherwise circulated in any form of binding or cover other than that in which it is published and without a similar condition being imposed on the subsequent purchaser.

All characters in this publication are fictitious and any resemblance to real persons, living or dead, is purely coincidental.

British Library Cataloguing in Publication Data

Adamoli, Vida
Sons, Lovers, Etcetera
1. English fiction – 20th century
I. Title
823.9'14 [F]

ISBN 0-7472-1794-7

Typeset by
CBS, Felixstowe, Suffolk

Printed in England by
Clays Ltd, St Ives Plc

HEADLINE BOOK PUBLISHING
A division of Hodder Headline PLC
338 Euston Road
London NW1 3BH

For Julian and Lucian

and all my beautiful family

Chapter 1

Rome. July 20. The slumbering hour just before dawn.

Kate awoke with a pounding heart to see the Angel of Death looming over her white starched bed. Its cowled head grazed the ceiling, and whispered incantations emanating from the cavernous mouth grew in tidal waves to drown her in hissing sound. 'This is it,' she thought, as its great wings spread. Then infinite darkness enveloped her.

Time, as they say, stood still.

When she resurfaced the overhead light had been switched on pinning her down with its ruthless glare. Slowly she shifted her gaze to a vase of funereal lilies on the bedside table, then contemplated the long, sorrowful face with stained tombstone teeth and a burst of grey whiskers on a sharp chin standing next to it. It wasn't, after all, the Angel of Death. It was Sister Luigina.

Kate arched her back, unclenched her jaw and let out a primal scream. The agonized sound bounced off the crucifix above the bed, ricocheted down the wide marble-floored corridor outside her room and lost itself in the outer reaches of the universe. Immediately the nun's bony fingers went into vigorous prodding action. '*Madonna santa! Aiuta questa povera creatura nella sua sofferenza!*' she cried. 'Where is it now, *cara*? Here? Here? Here?'

And well might she ask.

Kate had been languishing for over a week in the private clinic in Rome's exclusive Parioli quarter, hoping to discover the origin of a mysterious pain that roamed her body like a tormented vagabond. Sometimes it was in her chest, sometimes in her stomach, sometimes in her knee, often in her head and even, on occasions, in her left little finger. This time, however, the pain wasn't the cause of her agony. Or *that* pain, at least. It was staring into the sepulchral darkness behind Sister Luigina's thin lips and realizing there was no light at the end of the tunnel. Her scream trembled, then died. Or rather, like the genie in Aladdin's lamp, imploded into a hard little nugget and relodged itself behind her heart.

'A painkiller?' Sister Luigina lisped. 'A suppository? Or perhaps just a nice cup of camomile tea?' She wasn't, in fact, anything like the Angel of Death. She was a pious, good-hearted and well-meaning virgin. Kate returned the eager, busy hand.

Then she sat up, lit a cigarette and calculated just how much her stay at the Clinic of the Immaculate Conception had already cost her. If one included the rosemary rub-down, colonic irrigation, after-dinner brandies and other such essential extras, probably more than two weeks at the Seychelles Hilton. If there was a Hilton in the Seychelles.

'A suppository,' she said in voice so loud and hollow it startled them both. 'And then call me a taxi. I'm going home.'

The taxi arrived at 6.15. At 6.20 she was driving down the

Sons, Lovers, Etcetera

Via Veneto, past shuttered cafés and shops and three transvestite whores with ruined lipstick and crotch-grazing minis who looked like weary Fellini extras in the early sunlight. At 6.35 she was letting herself into her fourth-floor apartment, ready for the silence and stale reek of Nazionale cigarettes which rose to greet her. But there was more, of course.

Well, there always is, isn't there?

That more was the huge clamouring vortex that had appeared five months earlier when the cherished fruit of her womb left home – aged twenty-one – to live with his girlfriend. Like her mysterious pain the vortex was not located in any one place. It could appear while she prepared lunch, gave herself a face-pack or flicked a duster around Lorenzo's now empty room. And then down she'd go, a middle-aged Alice sucked into a red, throbbing, weeping, keening rabbit-hole. Sometimes the vortex would spit her up after an hour or so. Sometimes it held her captive for days.

It was a perilous existence.
She had always to be on the alert.

So she paused warily on the threshold. Then took a deep breath and tiptoed with tremulous caution down the corridor into the bedroom.

The shutters were tightly closed. It was dark and the air ripe with sweat and slumber. Despite limited visibility however, Kate immediately saw that there were two bodies in the bed where there should only have been one. The body with the greying beard and nominal chest hair was her husband, Daniele. The body with the tangled blonde mop, snoring wetly into his shoulder, was Louisa.

Louisa was a photographer on Daniele's paper and Kate knew her quite well. Or, to be more accurate, they'd met socially on several occasions. And twice, when visiting her mother who lived near by, Louisa had popped in for a coffee and a chat. She invariably wore trousers, T-shirts and an army camouflage jacket, cultivating an intrepid 'I've just got back from an assignment in San Salvador' look. It was a style Kate envied and wished she could carry off herself.

On both occasions she had found Kate ironing Daniele's shirts. And on both occasions Kate was hot, flushed and irritable. 'You want to know why I don't get married?' Louisa said in a tone that mixed pity with contempt. 'I'll tell you why, *cara*. Marriage is like a trick coin. Heads he wins, tails you lose. Always.'

Kate recalled this witticism as she looked at them now. Then she lifted the overnight case (containing nightdress, slippers, several tons of toiletries, an SF anthology, Jung's *Analytical Psychology* and a towel stolen from the clinic) and hurled it at their heads.

The time at that moment was precisely 6.40 and the day was already on its way to being a scorcher. As the hours progressed the temperature climbed to a feverish 105 degrees that had the entire city gasping. Violence shimmered in the glittering dust particles in the dry air and by evening newscasters were reporting assaults, suicides and the bizarre murder of an elderly German by his wife on the Spanish Steps. It was the second day of a holiday they'd been planning for years and that had been organized to coincide with their golden wedding anniversary. Eyewitnesses testified that the couple had been making a slow descent, the man aided by a walking stick, when for no apparent reason the frail old lady went berserk. She knocked him to his knees, then stabbed him in the throat severing his jugular vein. The murder weapon was a souvenir penknife with a picture of the Pope on the pearlized plastic handle. A relative, contacted in their home city of Munich, was quoted as saying they were 'a devoted couple and had always seemed very happy'.

Sehr gluchlich! Molto felice!

Kate watched this news item sprawled on the damp tiles of the living-room floor. She was naked except for knickers. Sweat beaded her nose, upper lip, trickled down her spine and coursed between her breasts to form a subtropical pool where hungry piranha fish swam in the deep hollow of her navel. She found the story riveting. It electrified her, in fact. Had it, she wondered, been a spontaneous reaction to a lifetime of bullying? Or was it patiently plotted revenge for an unspeakable cruelty inflicted in their distant past?

Like drunkenly raping her on their wedding night.
Like violating the secrets of her hidden diary.
Like sexually abusing their only daughter.

After a while, fantasies of killing Daniele began a delirious Technicolor dance in her head. They were hot, flame-licked pictures from the voodoo fire where she had once kept her heart. At her trial she would tell of the pain and humiliation his infidelities had always caused her. She would denounce him for turning the spirited English girl he'd married into a stateless woman neither of them were interested in. At her testimony judge and jury would weep rivers of blood and stars would spin in sympathy and

Vida Adamoli

outrage. And women past, present and future would rise from the earth to cheer and applaud her.

Hooray!

Chapter 2

But murder, sadly, had to wait.

Daniele – last seen trying to wrestle a hysterical Louisa into the lift – decided that in the circumstances he was better off staying with his mother. This suited him fine because he much preferred her cooking and furthermore, she always brought him morning coffee in bed. It also gave him the chance to play with an old electric train set which, to stop his son molesting, he preferred to keep in his boyhood room.

Lidia, a small, fat woman of the most traditional views, considered her son a cheating scoundrel like the rest of his sex. Nevertheless she had always advised her daughter-in-law to make expediency her measure and turn a blind eye to his dirty deeds. 'After all,' she counselled wisely when she phoned Kate after his dishevelled arrival on her doorstep. 'He's the foreign news editor now and earns good money. You've had to endure the lean years, why should some strumpet step in and get the cream?'

Lidia was fond of Kate and knew what she was talking about. She had put up with a philandering husband who kept her on a shoestring budget for forty-seven years. The first thing she did when the funeral was over was sell his valuable collection of Japanese erotica (which included seventeenth-century woodblock prints, phallic fetishes and high-gloss girlie magazines), buy herself a complete new wardrobe and take her favourite sister on a six-week luxury cruise. Now she spent most afternoons playing bridge and drinking Camparis with her cronies at the Café Dante.

As she often said, 'Widowhood is well worth waiting for.'

The undignified scene by the lift was witnessed by Maria, Kate's downstairs neighbour and only real friend. Also up at dawn, she was woken by her husband choking on bridgework that had come loose in the night. A thin man with a despondent walrus moustache, Fulvio immediately hung upside down on the exercise bar fitted across the top of the kitchen doorway but, despite the position and coughing himself dizzy, the teeth wouldn't budge. Maria had always known that Fulvio was not a brave man. This time, however, his terror that the prosthesis would cause a fatal rupture of his windpipe was so acute that she couldn't ignore his ravings as she usually did. In fact, she was obliged to get up and offer to drive him to the casualty department of San Giacomo. And considering that Maria regarded her sleep as sacred, this was quite something.

They were on the landing, Fulvio clinging to her arm for support, when they heard the sudden explosion of voices from the floor above. Maria peered up the stairwell to see Kate, Daniele and a distraught blonde, who at that moment was calling Kate a cow for flushing her contact lenses down the toilet. Daniele's flies gaped beneath the roll of his belly and his shirt flapped limply as he hopped around trying to force his left foot into his right shoe. 'She's mad!' he shouted. 'You're mad! All women are mad! This whole drama is being created out of deranged jealousy!'

Daniele was quite obviously in a state of shock and incoherent rage. His eyes were wild, the veins on his neck bulged, his arms flailed. Then just as he was gathering breath to continue the tirade, Louisa drew back her fist and socked him full in the mouth. It was a beautiful and superbly timed gesture. And Daniele was not the only one to be silenced.

The frame froze. Time and animation were magically suspended.

And, for a moment, Kate too was part of that stillness. Suddenly none of it seemed to have anything much to do with her. Daniele and Louisa were very small and far away, like two matchstick figures seen down the wrong end of a telescope. So she left them to it and went back inside. She didn't even slam the door behind her.

Later, shutters closed against the explosive heat, she watched television and worked her way through a bottle of chilled white wine – one of several good Frascatis with which Daniele had stocked the fridge. Over the next few days she ate little, drank much, thrashed around in the vortex and every now and then monitored her itinerant pain. She also did a lot of thinking about her life.

Or, rather, her routine, which was what her life had been principally about.

It went like this: 7 a.m. make breakfast and see husband/ son off to work/school. 7.50-9.30 a.m. housework – which three times a week included washing all tiled floors. 10 a.m. set off on two-mile trek to market (fruit, vegetables and bread bought fresh daily. Kate also followed the Roman tradition of serving chick-peas and salt cod every Friday.) Lunch, a serious affair, took at least an hour to prepare and just as long to clear up. When Lorenzo was little she took him to the nearby piazza every afternoon to play. Later it was sports activities and homework that had to be supervised.

Lorenzo! Lorenzino! Renzino!
Amore della mamma!

Since Lorenzo's departure Kate was aware that she underwent serious physiological disturbances at the mere sound of his name. Her lungs ballooned, her heart contracted and her womb seethed with the boiling lava of her passionate maternal love. Somewhere along the road – probably when he was about three – Lorenzo had become her monopolizing interest and, eventually, her only pride. His shining, beautiful face was the only mirror that reflected a picture of herself she could bear to acknowledge. Until he was twelve she concerned herself with his general psychological and physical health and school performance. During his teenage years she worried about his moral and physical safety, his enthusiasm for wanking and the fact that one day he'd leave her. Which, of course, he did. At the first opportunity.

And who, after all, could blame him?

Kate had not, of course, set out to make herself downtrodden and vulnerable. Well, nobody does, do they? When she married at eighteen during her final year at art school she did so for love – although the fact that she was pregnant also played a significant part. Romantic optimism was nevertheless flying high and it never occurred to her that life would be anything other than wonderful and exciting. (She also took it for granted that she would be a successful and admired painter.) Even her mother, a reasonably worldly woman, shrank from being a spoilsport and issuing a warning. Having failed to persuade her daughter to have an abortion, she limited herself to asking if the couple were compatible in bed.

The conversation took place during a salad lunch at Selfridges. 'It's my duty to ask you about the sex, darling,' she said in a sudden, strangled undertone. 'I mean, do you like doing it with him?' Kate and her mother enjoyed an open relationship. Such directness, however, coming as it did out of the blue, embarrassed Kate so much she dropped a forkful of sweetcorn and beetroot straight into her lap. Her mother took this confusion as an affirmative. 'Good,' she said, smiling wistfully. 'Because if that works, then everything will.'

Oh, really?

It wasn't until years later that Kate realized she had been given a glimpse of the darker currents working beneath the seemingly smooth surface of her parents' marriage. It prepared her to a certain extent for their subsequent divorce. But it sure as hell misled her about everything else.

That things weren't going to be quite as Kate expected became quickly apparent. She went to Italy in excited anticipation of great art, great wine and great suntans. Which, indeed, she got. But after a few months of living in two cramped rooms with no money, no friends and long days alone with a demanding baby, the attraction significantly palled. For a while she struggled to retain artistic fantasies but paint and canvases were beyond the budget, and after a couple of years she gave up. Then one day she awoke to find she was in a different place from the one she had thought she was in. She had joined a world of women for whom husband, children and home were the cardinal points of the common compass. A world where a woman's entire existence was shaped by her family needs.

And that was another beginning.

She started talking to herself (only at home, of course) when Lorenzo was still in nappies. It wasn't surprising really. After all, Daniele was out most of the time and there was only herself to have an adult conversation with. Around the same time she began indulging in gentle, comforting fantasies that centred around being fêted and admired. They were skilfully crafted, creative scenarios and for several years served her well. Gradually, however, as inspiration ran dry, they lost their power. And it was then that her dreams came into their own, obsessing her with their vivid intensity. In fact, more than dreams, they were the portal to a parallel existence. A parallel existence where heaven and hell fought for her soul. A parallel existence where she could break her chains and fly like a bird. A parallel existence from which she returned with her morning brain spinning like a Catherine wheel.

And as an escape from reality it was far less disruptive to the household than if she'd tried to get a job.

One of the consequences of the Louisa incident was that Kate's dream pattern changed: that is, it wasn't only happening at night. At any hour, and without warning, she found pictures from the deep recesses of her mind dropping like ripe purple plums into the lap of her unstable consciousness. She was visited by birth, death, sex, blood, gore, winged birds, Daniele, Lorenzo, Lidia, her mother, father – even the geography teacher who put his hand up her skirt when she was twelve. She was living the simultaneity of past, present and future and it was as perilous as the vortex.

In fact, it totally freaked her out.

'Daniele's right!' she sobbed to Maria, who was proving that a friend in need is a friend indeed. 'I am mad. More than mad – I'm out of my skull. I'm a clinical case and I need a straight-jacket.'

'You're not mad, you're drunk,' Maria said, very matter-of-fact, removing the bottle of Frascati out of Kate's reach. 'And it's quite understandable. This whole thing's a stinking mess.'

Although she was talking about Kate's marriage, she could also have been referring to the state of the flat. Kate had tipped Daniele's clothes into one big heap on the bedroom floor and taped his dirty socks and underpants in a frieze around the living-room walls.

'I'm dying,' Kate wailed. 'And there's nothing I can do about it.'

Maria, who frequently got drunk herself, was not dismayed. She also drew strength from the belief she had the gift of psychic powers – a belief that consistent prophetic failures could not shake.

'Yes there is,' she said firmly. 'You can come down to my place. I'll make you coffee and read your cards.'

Chapter 3

Kate always liked going to Maria's flat. Whereas her own apartment bordered on spartan, Maria's was an abundance of plush. It was a romantic's vision of a high-class bordello, with red velvet upholstery, silky tasselled drapes, gilt-framed mirrors, silver candlesticks, a pair of coy china nymphettes and paintings of more robust nudes (from the brush of a brother-in-law who worked in a bank) hanging on pink floral walls. The welcome this opulence extended was heightened by an underlying smell of talc mixed with the lingering fragrance of rosemary and garlic that always perfumed the air.

   Kate, who loved Maria like the sister she'd never had, thought it the perfect setting for her. It was the outward manifestation of her inner essence, declaring to all who entered her awesome potential as one of life's truly great sensualists. For in an ideal world Maria's days would be spent in a blissful orgy of eating, drinking, laughing and making love to men who – unlike Fulvio – were hung like horses. The reality, as it usually is, however, was sadly different.

In fact, if truth be told, it was a painful austerity.

Rarely a day went by when Maria wasn't trying to starve away the triple-tiered belly that sank softly towards her dimpled, billowing thighs. And despite tiny, see-through panties fringed with her crisp, abundant and unruly pubic hair, her erotic indulgences were restricted to nothing more than avid and expert crotch-watching. Unless, of course, one counted the occasions she rolled on to her back to fulfil her conjugal obligations. Which *she* definitely didn't.

They owed the start of their friendship to a tortoise briefly called Big Jim. Daniele had given it to Lorenzo on his eighth birthday and the same day it squeezed through the bars of their terrace to fall, miraculously unharmed, into Maria's below. It was scooped up by her five-year-old daughter, Lina, who put it into her doll's pram and immediately renamed it Tinkerbell. When Kate went down to reclaim the reptile she was met by a storm of tears. As she didn't have the heart to prise the creature from the small sobbing chest, she told Lina she could keep it and she would buy her little boy another one. (Lorenzo, however, admitted later that he didn't like tortoises and wanted a skateboard instead).

Radiantly triumphant, Lina dried her eyes and took Tinkerbell to her room where she pretended it was a baby and wrapped it in various bits of diaphanous material. Maria showed her gratitude for this generosity by producing a bottle of Marsala and some home-made macaroons. The first and second glass took them through the usual small talk. By the third, real warmth was beginning to manifest in their smiles. By the fifth they were roller-coasting. But it was Maria, with five sisters and an innate gift for female intimacy, who ultimately bridged their distance.

She brought up the subject of her malfunctioning intestines.

* * *

Sons, Lovers, Etcetera

Disappearing into her bedroom for a moment she returned with the large X-ray she had collected that very day from her doctor. 'There!' she cried, pointing to an undulating line of what looked like a string of white sausages floating in black broth. 'Can you see that twisted loop down there? I mean, have you ever seen anything like it?'

Kate, who was soon to discover that Maria was intensely interested in all bodily functions and knew Garzanti's *Medical Encyclopaedia* back to front, hadn't a clue what innards were supposed to look like. She kept this to herself, however, and to be accommodating agreed it did look very strange.

'Exactly! It's deformed,' Maria grabbed two large handfuls of flesh from her hips and shook them. 'That's why I'm fat – all my food gets stuck in that loop and rots there. It's so unfair! Nobody believes me when I say I eat like a bird.'

The effect of this penetrating and intimate view into the bowels of Maria's life was to make them instantly close. It also led to an earnest discussion on the relative merits of glycerine suppositories, prunes, senna pods and even surgery. It was a mutually satisfying and open exchange during which a deep and lasting bond was formed. When they made up their minds they liked each other. When the seeds of love and respect were sown.

The next time they met for a glass of Marsala the topic was breasts – volume, shape and consistency. Such was the underlying trust, Kate found herself confessing that hers had been both her greatest triumph and her first experience of grief. Quickly getting into her stride, she described how they had grown from inauspicious sproutings at the age of twelve into twin globes of wondrous perfection. ('A great pair of knockers' was how they were frequently described.) She pinpointed the moment of their full flowering to her eighteenth birthday

– a month before Lorenzo was conceived – when they all but burst out of the lacy 36C bra which had been one of her presents. A year later – baby now on the bottle – they had shrunk to a 34B and their buoyant glory was gone. For Kate this had been her first chilling insight into the transient nature of all things.

It was devastating on a cosmic scale.
It also taught her that grief is very lonely.

Daniele came home one day to find her weeping into a sinkful of soiled baby clothes. 'If I think they're OK, what are you worried about?' he said, doing his best to be reassuring and sympathetic. 'Unless, of course, you're planning on having an affair. Ha, ha!'

And now, twenty years on, drunk and disorderly, she was crying about breasts again. Only it was Louisa's breasts this time. 'They're small and round,' she whimpered. 'And her nipples are like those fat glacé cherries my grandmother used to stick in the middle of custard tarts.'

Maria, a woman who favoured loose smocks beneath which her own large mammaries could swing free, was not impressed. 'In my experience,' she said, patting Kate's hand, 'flat-chested women are either lesbians or nymphomaniacs. And even if they're not, you can take it from me they're always bad news.'

Quite!

She gave her a tissue to blow her nose and went into the kitchen to see about the coffee. Kate crumpled it in her hand, sniffed deeply, and slumped back in the armchair. Above her head a pair of mating bluebottles spun an ecstatic dance in the hot, breathless air. Buzz-buzz-buzz. Love in Action. Love Making the World Go Round. What a joke. What a con. What a can of worms! It made her sick.

'As of today I'm giving up sex,' she announced when Maria returned with a tray. 'I should have done it years ago. I was never much good at it, and you just have to think of the Third World to see it's the root cause of all our misery.'

Maria, however, despite the martyrdom of her marital bed, could not endorse such blasphemy, even to humour her friend. She handed Kate a cup of strong black coffee and pointed out that she must remember she was not only drunk, she was also 'very depressed'.

Kate nodded. 'I am depressed,' she agreed solemnly. 'My husband is a selfish, autocratic, insensitive womanizer and I'm his doormat. My only child has left home and no longer needs me. I'm a domestic skivvy with no marketable skills, no self-respect and no prospects. I am forty years old, I no longer have beautiful breasts and I haven't a clue how to salvage what's left of my life.'

So there!

They lit up contraband Marlboros (supplied by another brother-in-law who worked for the railway) and polished off a plate of cheese straws. Then Maria cleared a space on the coffee table and got out her tarot. They'd done this many times before so Kate was well acquainted with the procedure. While she shuffled and laid out the cards, Maria closed her eyes and communed with her higher psychic self. One minute passed, then two, then five. Maria opened her eyes, breathed deeply, and gazed intently at the spread. '*Mio dio*! Look at it! Just look at the chaos and confusion!' she exclaimed. 'And there's something very big looming on the horizon. An unexpected and drastic change to your circumstances. Not to worry, though. There is no doubt the outcome will be to your definite advantage.'

Visions of glorious widowhood along the lines of that enjoyed by Lidia sprang into Kate's mind. 'Is Daniele going to die?' she asked eagerly. 'In a car crash, perhaps? His sternum crushed by the steering wheel? I mean, it would make sense. He's such a reckless and aggressive driver.'

Maria shook her head regretfully. 'No, *cara*, I'm afraid not. This concerns a journey, one that will take you across the sea. And it will be a woman who stretches out a helping hand.'

'My mother! She's inviting me to spend an expenses-paid holiday with her in Tel Aviv.'

'No, it's not your mother. This woman's very tall and dark and she's no relation.'

Kate slumped back in the chair, lit another cigarette and stared at the bluebottles again. That she found the reading uninspiring and comfortless was quite obvious. 'Listen,' Maria said defensively. 'You can believe it or not, it's up to you. But I'm telling you, it's not just the cards. I'm getting strong telepathic feedback.'

Maria's telepathic ability was as notoriously unspectacular as the rest of her clairvoyant skills. This time, however, her prediction proved to be absolutely correct. Two weeks later Kate bought a one-way plane ticket to London, packed her bags and left Daniele.

For ever.

Chapter 4

In fact, Maria got it almost – not absolutely – right. Her prediction erred on one minor (and totally unimportant) point. And that was that Heather could not be called dark. Her skin was of a typically rosy, Anglo-saxon hue and her mouse-brown hair – first bleached at fourteen – had since run the spectrum from platinum to caramel blonde. And on her thirty-seventh birthday the chill of encroaching middle age sent her running to the hairdresser to have it streaked pink and green. It was a Day-Glo mistake she never repeated.

She was tall, however. In fact, it was her height Kate first noticed when the headmistress ushered her in to join Miss Jackson's class of twelve-year-olds – that and the crowning indignity of her mother's anxious kiss tattooed in hideous wine red on her blushing cheek. Thirty pairs of malicious eyes stared as she shuffled head down and miserable to a desk by the leaking radiator at the back of the room. She was already five-foot seven, ungainly, and pubescent fat warped the razor-sharp pleats of her new navy skirt. By the time she left three years later with four O levels – and the reputation for being the best netball player the school had ever had – she was five-eleven and prayed desperately every night to stop growing.

She claimed it was the only prayer Him Up There had ever bothered to answer.

Vida Adamoli

* * *

For the first term Kate tortured her with a sadism most of us learn in nursery school and spend the rest of our scholastic life refining. At a certain point during the second term, however, they became Best Friends. Or, to put it another way, fellow surfers who rode the turbulent waves of adolescence together. This switch in their relationship started with an argument over a Mars bar at a bus stop and was subsequently consolidated by a shared passion for boys, the Beatles, erotic speculations and dreams of perfect love.

The usual things.

Then Kate got married and left for Italy, leaving Heather to embark on her nomadic path through a succession of jobs, relationships and rented accommodation in north London. But despite their different destinies they always made the effort to keep in touch. The reason for this was not so much affection – although there was that, too – but an envious attraction for what they both believed the other's life to be. Kate fantasized jealously about the excitement and opportunities enjoyed by an unattached girl-about-town. Heather, on bleak Sundays (and especially during periods of enforced celibacy), longed to be a wife and mother with a terrace of riotous geraniums and long months of Mediterranean sun. She also had the wild notion, deeply resented by Kate, that housewives spent most of the time with their feet up doing nothing.

   The odd card or phone call, meeting for lunch on the increasingly rare occasions Kate took a trip home, kept these fantasies alive. By virtue of this tenuous association, they were able to nurture the vicarious feeling that something of what the other had was also theirs.

Sons, Lovers, Etcetera

* * *

The day Heather called was almost as hot as the day the German tourist was stabbed on the Spanish Steps. To make matters worse a broken mains had left the Monte Verde quarter, where Kate lived, without water (she had showered the previous evening, pouring two bottles of fizzy mineral water over her head). She hadn't left the flat for over a week, and what little food she had forced herself to eat was delivered by her local *alimentari* and left outside the front door. Most of the time she was prisoner of both her pain – now lodged deep in her belly – and the terrible, terrifying vortex. On that particular morning the vortex claimed her as soon as she tried to get out of bed. So, sensibly, she turned over and went straight back to sleep again.

It was a dense, multi-strata slumber and it took a while for the persistent ringing of the phone to drill through. When it did she struggled to consciousness like a drowning woman fighting a vicious undertow. The line was bad and Heather's voice rose and fell on waves of static. It sounded as if she was calling from the dark side of the moon – which to Kate, marooned on a rocky island of no escape, she might just as well have been.

When they had last spoken some eight months earlier, Heather was talking about opening a vegetarian café with two girlfriends and had hinted at a lesbian liaison. Now it was to tell her that in the space of five weeks she had met and married (in white, at Chelsea town hall), a rich American art dealer with whom she was flying to New York that very weekend. This had happened at a moment, she said roaring with laughter, when life had lost its meaning and she was debating whether to take a barbiturate overdose or put her head in the gas oven.

'It was a bloody miracle,' she said. 'Know what I mean?'
Kate didn't reply.

'Kate? Are you there?'

It took a supreme effort to prise her dry tongue from the roof of her dry mouth. 'Yes,' she croaked when the difficult operation had been achieved, 'I'm here.'

'Look, my sweets, I know this is a terrible line but you don't sound quite right. Is anything the matter?'

Because of her dominant role in their girlhood, Kate was always aware that she held the edge of power in their relationship. And even now, on her knees and bleeding, there was something that still did not want to let that go. It was a tattered rag of pathetic pride, but she fought for it. And fought hard, too, before the dam broke and the swell of her grief washed over both of them.

Which certainly rewrote the fantasy a bit. Being a trooper, however, Heather took it in her stride.

'Listen,' she said. 'Remember when I was involved with that junkie and he fucked me over so badly I had to spend three months in Scotland getting my head straight? OK, the circumstances are slightly different, but it's basically the same shit. The bottom line is that when you live in a toilet you get used to the stink. You have to get out to realize just how bad it is – and you can take that on trust from someone who's been neck-high in faeces all her life!' She roared again, an explosion of crackle in Kate's pained ear.

'Now then, I had more or less agreed to sublet my flat to the daughter of a neighbour. But that's OK. She's a disgustingly spoiled brat and I don't owe her anything. You're my friend and I want you to take it instead. It's not Buckingham Palace, but it's dirt cheap and you need the breathing space. Yes or no now, sweetpea. I'm not leaving it empty for squatters.'

For once Kate did not flounder in an agony of indecision. A moment of lucid wisdom revealed the offer for the lifeline it was. It also occurred to her, given that Maria had so triumphantly predicted this with the cards, that this was Fate in Action. It was the verification of a Mystic Plan. They sorted out a few small details (like the exact address, where Kate could pick up the keys, etc.), then Heather said, 'Isn't life funny? I mean, doesn't it strike you as ironic that I should take a husband just as you are leaving yours? And that I'm leaving London at the precise moment you're returning?'

Hmmm.
Quite.

Daniele insisted on driving Kate to the airport. It was his way of diminishing the significance of her departure, a refusal to acknowledge there was any real problem outside that of her own making. He certainly refused to believe this was the end of their marriage. In his eyes her flight to London was a histrionic, attention-grabbing gesture designed to punish him and bring him to heel. 'And if you think you can solve your problems geographically you are simply being absurd,' he told her. Furthermore, as a proud Latin of the old order, the thought of any woman bringing him to heel made him angry and defensive. Sometimes it also seemed so preposterous it made him laugh.

The traffic was heavy, making it a slow, sweaty drive. Daniele chain-smoked and kept his hand impatiently on the hooter. Then, while trying to cut from one congested lane to another, he grazed the gleaming bumper of a flame-red Alfa Romeo in front. Although there was no visible damage, the possibility that there might have been sent the other driver into a paroxysm of fury. There was a bellowing, ten-minute confrontation in the middle of the road that only just stopped short of actual blows. *"Sto stronzo!"* Daniele muttered when he got back in the car. His mood had been bad from the outset. He had indulged in a large, very good lunch at the Tuscan restaurant round the corner from his office and all he wanted now was a long siesta.

Kate, on the other hand, hadn't eaten a proper meal since the Louisa incident. Maria had frequently tried to tempt her with the succulent delicacies of her kitchen, to no avail. That very day she had brought her an exquisite dish of stewed tripe with olives. It was an offering anointed with grieving tears, but Kate had been unable to manage more than a couple of dutiful mouthfuls.

To say that Maria was heartbroken at Kate's departure was no exaggeration. They were bonded in a sisterhood nourished daily by the shared minutiae of their domestic existence. And to lose it was to be for ever bereft.

'I'll miss you,' Maria wept as they clung to each other in poignant farewell. 'But I'm proud of you, too. I never thought you could be so brave.'

It was a nice thing to say but neither of them believed it. They both knew perfectly well that, like someone on a fatally crippled aircraft, Kate's only option was to jump.

'Ticket? Passport? Money? Better make sure you haven't forgotten something. You usually do.' Daniele crushed his cigarette into the overflowing ashtray, determined to play the controlling husband to the last. From force of habit, from self-doubt, and possibly because she found comfort in this re-enactment of a familiar pattern, Kate obediently opened her bag and checked.

Ticket. Passport. Money. It was all there. She glanced at Daniele's grim profile and remembered when he had been a lean-angled man whose wide, green-flecked eyes, lopsided smile and outrageous wit had charmed the pants off her. But that was long ago. She thought of her bedroom as she had left it: shuttered and cool with the book she'd decided at the last minute not to take tossed on the patchwork bedspread. It stayed in her mind's eye as a frozen tableau, an image already lost to another lifetime.

Turning her head, she found herself staring at her ghostly reflection in the side window's dirt-splattered glass. It was surreal, insubstantial as a faded transparency. The reflection of a person who had ceased to exist.

At that moment Kate, too, had a psychic premonition.

'Oh, my God,' she thought, with sudden certainty. 'This is the end of my life. When I get to London, I'll die.'

Chapter 5

Kate didn't die, of course, but she did have a rather nasty landing.

She was sitting next to a young man wearing a red Lacoste T-shirt and Wayfarer sunglasses who kept his nose stuck in the *Corriere dello Sport* throughout the entire flight. His concentration faltered when they started the descent and the plane ripped through strata of low-flying cloud like a screeching banshee to bump, grind and scrape its belly along the Heathrow tarmac. At the jarring moment of impact he crushed the newspaper between locked knees and seized Kate's hand – a vicelike grip that pinched a nerve and sent a shooting pain up her arm. '*Porca Madonna!*' he gasped when they finally came to a standstill. '*Cos'è? Un bevenuto a Londra?*'

They looked at each other properly for the first time. Kate saw a fresh-faced youth of about Lorenzo's age, all neat and polished on the sleeve of maternal devotion. He saw a woman with mascara running in black streaks from swollen, bloodshot eyes. The sight of her distress instantly dispelled his panic and brought out the man in him. 'Please,' he said earnestly, releasing her hand. 'Don't worry about a thing. It's all right. I will help you.'

After gallantly producing a refresher towelette, he then proceeded to tell her all about himself. His name, he said as they shuffled down the aisle, was Marcello and he was a law student at Bologna University. He had no intention of practising, however, as he wanted to be a movie actor and live in New York. He also said the reason he wanted to escort her safely into London was because she reminded him of his mother (who, he confided shyly, also cried a lot).

Unfortunately this was not to be.

On their way through Nothing to Declare, they were stopped by a customs officer who quickly found the large lump of hash Marcello had wrapped in tin foil and stashed inside a pair of socks. As they were together, both Kate's luggage and person were also subjected to meticulous investigation. The woman officer who carried out the body search was a curly-haired Liverpudlian with a plump, ruby-red smile. 'So,' she said, when the indignity was over. 'What's your relationship to that young man, then?'

Kate snatched her dress back off the hook. 'What relationship? I met the poor bugger on the plane.'

'Well, well!' the officer said, adding insult to injury with an impudent wink. 'It's a shame we had to take him away from you so soon, then, isn't it? Better luck next time, dearie.'

And that was the second time in twenty-four hours someone had said that to her. Louisa was the first.

Louisa had disturbed Kate in the middle of her fraught packing to apologize for the part she had played in the whole traumatic affair. But even if Kate hadn't caught them in bed together, she pointed out, Daniele was such a disgusting male chauvinist, that Kate should have left him years ago. She also added that, like all men into power trips, he was a lousy screw. 'It's good riddance to bad rubbish, believe me,' she said. 'I hope you have better luck next time.'

Kate's response was a bitter laugh. 'Next time' was a totally incomprehensible combination of words. It was a non-existent concept, a mythical landing stage floating somewhere in the vast sea of tomorrow's grey eternity.

And who, for God's sake, would want to contemplate that?

Due to the trouble at customs, Kate arrived at the basement flat off the Holloway Road at eight p.m. – not six, as expected. Usually a sedate little cul-de-sac, it was, at that moment, in ferment. About fifteen people were gathered around two policemen who were busy taking notes. The atmosphere was tense and angry and one young woman with a toddler in a pushchair was verging on hysteria. It was, it seemed, a day for tears.

'That rapist has struck again, I'll bet. The one who does evil things with broomhandles and bottles and such like,' the taxi driver said darkly, shaking his large bald head as he counted out Kate's change. 'I mean, this is his area of operation, so to speak, ain't it? What with his last victim living just round the corner in Liverpool Road and all. I've got a friend who works in the hospital where she was recovering and he told me it took three hours to remove the broken glass from the poor girl's rear end.'

As it turned out, however, the agitation had nothing to do with the rapist (who waited four months before attacking again, and then it was in the Kilburn area). What had happened was that, earlier in the afternoon, a woman snatched a baby from her pram in the front garden of a house in the next road. It was reported that night on the late news and for the next seventy-two hours the entire nation held its breath. When the abductress was finally arrested, and little Jessica returned, it was a joyful reunion for mother and baby. For the soberly dressed blonde woman (filmed hiding her face at the back of a police car), however, it was a moment of crushing despair. She had a history of personal disasters and had recently suffered a miscarriage. The psychoanalyst and social psychologist who saw her soon after she was taken into custody said she had a deeply distorted sense of self-worth. Her whole perception of her identity had become dependent on becoming a mother. He pleaded for compassion, not a prison sentence.

The trauma of miscarriage, he declared, should never be undervalued.

Kate responded to these words from the depths of her being. After all, who better than herself to know their truth? For when first Rome, then Italy, slipped away in a turbo roar beneath her, she had miscarried nothing less than twenty years of her life. Her status, identity, all the roles which had defined her were stripped away and trailed in bloody shreds through the milky stratosphere. It had come to her then that her whole life had been an illusion, a long hallucinogenic dalliance in a fairground hall of fractured mirrors. And the pain of it was only partially anaesthetized by the consumption of several duty-free gin and tonics.

She was fragile and frightened. She was suffering from post-abortion anguish. Furthermore, it was to take her several weeks to get used to Heather's hard and lumpy bed.

Heather's flat was poky, crumpled and welcomed Kate

with the discarded debris of her absent presence. Clothes still hung in the wardrobe, furry, blue, boiled potatoes lurked forgotten at the back of the fridge, tendrils of gingery pubic hair clung with limpet tenacity to the side of the stained bath and odd bits of shabby underwear kept turning up everywhere. There was also a black cat – which Heather said in her note she had christened Mad Max – who had taken to occupying the small back garden between the hours of eleven and three each day. Whom he belonged to, she said, and where he spent the rest of the times was a mystery.

Kate didn't particularly like cats, but her new situation made her responsive to the animal's presence. For his part Mad Max was clearly not too sure how he felt about humans. He refused any food Kate offered, shrank if she tried to stroke him, but was not averse to a more spiritual rapport. To this end they established a daily ritual in which she lay on the grass next to him and they stared deeply into each other's eyes. She also talked to him, in Italian and mostly about Lorenzo when he was little, which he seemed to like. Some of the anecdotes were funny, others touching. And there were those she wasn't quite sure had really happened, or if they existed only in her imagination.

Every one of them, however, made her cry.

Kate got the feeling that Mad Max responded with particular attention to the story of Lorenzo, aged four, returning inconsolable from the nursery because a little girl had told him boys couldn't have babies. Her name was Teresa and Kate had been disturbed by the child's precocious maternal fixation. Not content with tending dolls – which she mostly dismembered – she was forever stuffing pillows and things into her knickers and pretending she was pregnant.

Another reason Kate worked on her relationship with the cat was because she knew no one in London any more and had nobody else to talk to. Her mother lived in Tel Aviv with her second husband, a gynaecologist, and her father had been killed a year after their divorce (by a piece of guttering falling from the roof of the Queen's Arms pub in Cricklewood and landing on his head). Her only brother, Walter, had given up a career in advertising to become an organic farmer in Wales. Not that she wished they were around. Her father had never much liked her after she ceased being his pretty little girl and became an overgrown stranger in tight skirts and tarty make-up whose primary interests were loud pop music and boys. Walter, eight years younger, had been an unwelcome shock when he arrived and an inconsequential presence ever after. Her mother, Miss Blackpool 1943, was well-meaning but neurotic. All her life she had suffered from a heart made restless by suppressed longings. And unable to control her heart, she made a point of controlling her environment instead.

She was a demon cleaner.

When Kate thought of her mother she thought of her maniacal hoovering, her troubled eyes raking the fawn pile of their immaculate living-room carpet like laser beams. And it didn't stop there. She polished banisters, picture frames, the undersides of tables and the back of the rug chest in the hall. Every surface shone with waxed brilliance and perfumed the air with an evangelical scent of lavender. She even scoured the lavatory with vocational fervour. It was order and hygienic rigour in place of love and adventure. In place of a meaning to life. And with the passing of time it got worse. Daniele hated it when they were invited to stay. He referred to her parents' home as a semi-detached sterile zone.

Around thirty, Kate was dismayed to discover just how much like her mother she had become. She was also a repository of suppressed yearnings and she, too, found housework a useful siphon. In her own home, however, mind and body worked in tandem performing routine domestic tasks with robotic efficiency. But in Heather's flat, where everything was unfamiliar, she was like a disabled person fumbling in the dark. Even a simple task like making a cup of tea took three times as long.

Another problem was shopping, usually done at a small shop round the corner. Clutching her wire basket she would gaze with bemused indecision at the edible merchandise ranged on the shelves: pappy-soft white sliced bread, bottles of Technicolor fruit squashes, tins of mushy peas and cream soups, instant mashed potato, obscene confections of fat, sickly pink sausages, slabs of cellophane-wrapped yellow and orange cheese. Used as she was to the glorious abundance of Italian markets, the mouth-watering magnificence of the food shops, she simply did not know what to buy. Once she tried a frozen steak and kidney pie which gave her ghastly diarrhoea. Usually she just settled for baked beans.

'Ah, beans! Very nice. Very nice indeed,' the Indian proprietor said on the day she stocked up with twenty-five tins. 'I would indulge myself but for a little problem. Air in the intestines,' he patted a distended belly clad in an electric blue shirt. 'My wife finds it very offensive, you know.'

Kate did know. 'Farty-pants,' Walter had once called her in the presence of a new boyfriend. It was one of those moments she still recalled with an indelible sense of shame. Her new single status, however, meant concerns of that sort were now behind her. She could fire away and nobody would care.

Without conscious effort she found that her days began to assume an established routine. She cleaned the flat, communed with Mad Max, shopped for and ate her beans. Sometimes in the late evening she took a slow stroll around the neighbourhood looking in other people's windows. This novel and compelling pursuit had not been possible when she had been growing up in London. Then an Englishman's home was truly his castle and domestic life was conducted behind the decorous drape of tightly drawn curtains. But now some windows had become giant TV screens, bright stage sets of stripped pine, Habitat furniture and rampant house-plants that offered a selection of scenarios for her attention.

It was with their tacit consent, she felt, that she violated the occupants' privacy. More than that, in fact. She instinctively perceived that their domiciliary displays needed – were even eager for – her questing eyes. And occasionally, while eating, entertaining, yawning, kissing, quarrelling, casually scratching an armpit or a backside, someone would glance out and stare straight at her. Or, more accurately, straight through her. It was an odd sensation and made her feel that she wasn't really there at all.

Like the shadow of a shadow.
Or a solitary presence in someone else's dream.

Or simply a lonely middle-aged woman with no one and no place to call her own.

Chapter 6

Window-gazing (spying, if you like) was but one of various new pursuits Kate now indulged in. For since arriving in London, it was continually revealed to her that things she believed constant and familiar actually possessed strange and hitherto unsuspected aspects. Indeed, it was being enlightened to this fact that compelled her to spend long hours examining her face in the mirror.

These contemplations had nothing to do with conventional vanity. They were inspired, instead, by an urgent need to reacquaint herself with features that, during the upheaval of recent events, seemed to have undergone a subtle change. Her eyes, for example, were definably narrower and a darker shade of grey; the curve of her nostrils had more flare; her cheekbones were sharper. She was leaner, more abstracted, more mysterious. Kate knew, of course, that these surface manifestations were just clues to a deeper reality. Like a painstaking and diligent archaeologist she probed beneath the layer of skin and muscle in search of the long-buried, long-forgotten presence that would make sense of it all. It was a fascinating and self-indulgent quest. It was also entertaining, as Heather invariably turned up to help her.

Heather might have conveniently moved herself to New York, but her projection – although technically spectral – was more solid than Kate herself.

* * *

The first time her friend materialized (in the bathroom where the sessions took place) Kate had been totally unfazed. Quite the contrary, in fact. It seemed to her the most natural – not to say appropriate – way to revive the easy intimacy of those preening, romantic years, when lipstick and mascara marked the great divide. When the shackles of childhood were dropping away in readiness for the dizzying plunge into adult life. Indeed, Kate could not imagine their relationship going so swimmingly in any other circumstances. Her defences were down. Her tongue was free of all restrictions. Conversation flowed between them as it had not done in more than twenty years.

Or, to be more accurate, the complaints did.

'It's not fair,' she said crossly to Heather that first day (they were both peering into the mirror while Kate investigated the fine lines bracketing her mouth). 'I wanted an unconventional life. I wanted to fill my days with excitement and adventure. You were the one who wanted to play Happy Families, not me!'

Heather moved to the loo, where she perched cross-legged and began examining her hair for split ends. A shrug of her shoulders acknowledged that this was true. 'It's the fault of those fairy godmothers whose job it is to make the dreams of teenage girls come true,' she said. 'The problem is, ours were either deaf or they seriously fucked up. The result, as you've just pointed out, my sweets, is that we each got landed with each other's gift pack. Still,' she wrinkled her nose philosophically. 'There's no point grizzling about it now, is there?'

But Kate was in grizzling mode.

'And what about sex?' she demanded. 'What about crashing waves and firework displays? What about swooning ecstasy and the erotic explosion of the senses? I was led to believe that the columned portal to cosmic bliss lay between semen-stained sheets.'

Heather, cross-eyed from the close inspection of a strand of hair, gave a rich chuckle. 'Weren't we all, darling. Weren't we all.'

It was the discovery of a copy of *Lady Chatterley's Lover* (last read aged fourteen) in Heather's bookcase that started Kate thinking about sex again. They were not lascivious thoughts, but more of a confused and uncertain meditation on the state of her atrophied libido. Along the lines of: would she ever feel the urge to do it again? And if she did, would she get the opportunity? Both prospects seemed extremely unlikely and the fact of their unlikeliness was a cold, dark presence at the back of her mind. Which, predictably, beckoned Maria in.

It was a late Saturday afternoon three weeks or so after Kate's arrival in London. She had spent the day in the garden talking to Mad Max, picking snails off irises and enjoying the sun's intermittent appearance from behind drifting castles of cloud. An added diversion was provided by the couple in the garden next door, who were discussing the extramarital affair of one of their friends. The husband (tactlessly Kate thought) commented that the woman in question had a great body. Instantly realizing his mistake he added that, personally speaking, overly curvaceous females – especially in the chest region – left him cold. This clumsy appendix, however, clearly did not convince.

'She's a maggot,' the wife bit back shrilly (Kate had seen her weeding the garden in shorts and a T-shirt. She was straight up and down like an ironing board.) 'She feeds off other people's lives. She's rotten to the stinking core!'

The conversation sprung instant barbs, soon reaching the point where they needed privacy to unleash the full potential of their marital arsenal. The wife stalked back inside, leaving the husband to trip over a portable radio as he stumbled after her. Kate heard him say 'Fuck!', then 'Bloody stupid cow!', after which the French windows were slammed shut and the rest of their exchange became frustratingly muffled. At which point Kate, too, went back inside, curled up on the sofa with D. H. Lawrence and promptly fell asleep.

Within seconds she was lying on the pavement outside Heather's flat copulating with a grunting, snorting, hunchbacked dwarf. When a curious passer-by paused to inquire politely if she was doing it out of pity, she replied sharply, 'Not at all. I want it too.' The dwarf then metamorphosed into a dark-skinned youth wearing tight blue jeans and a pair of silver court shoes with six-inch stiletto heels to boost his height.

'Good boy,' Kate crooned, stroking his smooth, hairless cheek. 'Now people will think you're almost normal.'

At which point the message of the dream was communicated to her in large red neon letters. They read: THIS IS YOUR FEMININITY.

The shock of this revelation tore her awake. She opened her eyes and at that precise moment Maria (in reality preparing her family's evening meal in Rome) popped up in front of her like the naughty surprise in a giant birthday cake. She was attired in the matching lacy bra and panties they had bought together several months earlier on a shopping spree in the Via del Corso.

'*Ciao!*' she said, grinning from ear to ear. 'I've come to tell you all about the amazing orgasm I had this morning.'

* * *

So! It was to be sex, sex and more sex!
But Kate did not mind. She was just overjoyed to see her.

'It happened after a blazing row with the paranoid inadequate it's my misfortune to have for a husband,' Maria said, lighting a Marlboro and smiling affectionately at her through a haze of cigarette smoke. 'At a certain point I stormed out of the flat, jumped into the car and set off to see my eldest sister, Betta, who has moved to San Lorenzo. I was beside myself. My anger was like a forest fire, scorching my mind, shrivelling my retina and rendering me blind. And then, out of the blue, it happened. Just as I pulled up at the traffic lights at the junction between Via Taormina and Piazza Doria. My blood boiled, my tendons snapped, my bones buckled and split open. It was, *cara amica*, a seismic eruption. I peaked just as the lights changed and collapsed like a broken doll over the steering wheel. At that moment the long line of cars behind began honking in unison. My ears rang with this numinous sound. Kate, you must believe what I'm telling you. It was nothing less than God's heavenly trumpeters heralding the Glory of my Coming!'

Wow!
Now that was more like it!

There was a moment of silence while they meditated on the wonder of this miracle. Then Maria folded her arms beneath her magnificent cleavage and gave Kate a pointed look.
  'So,' she demanded sternly. 'When did *you* last have an orgasm then?'
  'Good question,' Kate replied.

It had been, she recalled, after a tenants' meeting convened shortly after Christmas to discuss the problem of their new Sardinian porter (a maliciously deranged man who told kids he was a werewolf and regularly stranded tenants between floors by cutting off the power to the lift). The meeting ended around ten-thirty, after which Daniele ate a prosciutto and Gorgonzola sandwich, then carefully clipped his toenails on to the business section of *La Reppublica*. Once in bed, however – almost certainly inspired by two hours of sitting thigh to thigh on the settee with the provocative divorcee from flat 2 – he became quite lusty. Kate, by then tired and irritable, was not aroused by his attentions. So she turned to thoughts of an early boyfriend, Bernie Marks, to jolly things along.

The scene selected for replay was the occasion they had done it in a derelict house *en route* to a party in Camden Town. Hand in hand, picking their way through debris and rubbish to what had once been the kitchen, they consummated the act on a semi-collapsed trestle table. At the time the experience had been quite off-putting – partly because of the stench of urine, but mostly because of the large nail sticking in the softest and most vulnerable part of her bottom. Fortunately for her subsequent sex life, however, it had gained in erotic lustre ever since.

It wasn't the copulation itself but the memory of her youthful seductiveness and the effect of her clinging purple dress on Bernie's juvenile hormones that really turned Kate on.

'It cost twelve pounds from Neatawear,' she told Maria with a wistful sigh. 'And that was a lot of money for me then. But it was worth every penny. I looked unbelievably voluptuous.'

Maria had followed the story with great interest. 'Well,' she exclaimed. 'What are you waiting for? Go out and buy a purple dress right now! After all, you've got to start somewhere. And who knows, a new dress could be the first step to reclaiming your life.'

Hmm. Interesting thought.

Kate shut her eyes and began flicking through significant items of her past wardrobe. Imprinted on her closed lids she saw each outfit once again in catalogue-bright detail. There was the blue taffeta party dress with puffed sleeves and the sash that her mother made when she was eight; a tiered net petticoat Auntie Connie brought back from a trip to America; a blouse with zigzag patterns which she got as a thirteenth birthday present and, of course, the white corduroy trouser suit she wore on her first proper date with Daniele. It was a beautiful trouser suit but she made the mistake of wearing it with a pair of black, rather masculine loafers. When Daniele saw her arriving at the cinema in Notting Hill Gate he burst out laughing.

'You look like an ice-cream salesman,' he guffawed. 'A charming, *bella* ice-cream salesman, of course.'

She also remembered a three-quarter-length coat in dark green corduroy, a pleated mini that showed her knickers when she bent over Lorenzo's pram, a fluffy red monkey jacket with quarterback shoulders and a blue belt with silver buckle that Daniele had bought her back from a working trip to Guatemala.

'And what about the pink bikini,' Maria reminded her, lighting another cigarette. 'You haven't mentioned that.'

Ah, the pink bikini!
The itsy-bitsy teeny-weeny stretchy sexy pink bikini!

The pink bikini belonged to the year she and Lorenzo spent July and August in a tiny coastal village halfway between Rome and Naples (Daniele, busy with the paper, joined them at weekends). It was 1979, the year Mother Teresa received the Nobel Prize, Mrs Thatcher became Britain's first woman prime minister, Lorenzo broke his arm playing football and she celebrated her thirtieth birthday. More importantly, it was the year Kate embarked on her first affair, thereby ending more than a decade of one-sided fidelity. Maria had heard the story many times, but was always more than eager to hear it again.

'Go on,' she urged. 'Tell me about it.'

Smiling happily, Kate obliged.

Pietro was Sicilian, short, supple, with dark skin, black curly hair and intense blue eyes. He arrived on the beach each morning with three left-wing newspapers and a volume of Petrarch's poetry (in Latin to make sure everyone knew how cultured he was). Initially he just watched her from the shade of his umbrella, communicating his predatory interest with burning looks that skimmed like Frisbees over the incandescent sand. After five days of this (intensely erotic) foreplay he took action.

'You are a beautiful woman,' he stated authoritatively, accosting her at the water's edge. 'And this is no banal compliment. I'm an artist. I know what I'm talking about.'

(Which, indeed, he was. He painted large bleached-out canvases of windows opening on to empty vistas of sea and sky. He painted bleached-out canvases of books in bookcases, too.)

'You must come to my house and I will prepare a feast for you. We shall eat under the olive trees in the garden. I will make *zuppa di pesce*, roast peppers and my special peach and melon sorbet.'

'But I can't,' babbled Kate, breathless with excitement and panic. 'I'm married and the mother of an almost adolescent child.'

'That,' Pietro replied firmly, 'is of no consequence at all.'

And he was right, of course. It wasn't.

That very night they feasted under the olive trees on *zuppa di pesce*, roast peppers and peach and melon sorbet. Just as Pietro said they would. Afterwards he stroked her hair, nuzzled her neck, put an arm around her waist and led her to the bouncy bed in the corner of his charmingly untidy studio. For the next few hours they cleaved, clung and sweated in blissful copulation. He was forty-five years old with the vigour of a man twenty years younger. He took her three times in succession with scarcely a pause for breath. At two a.m., exhausted with pleasure, she roused herself to leave. But Pietro pulled her back on top of him, kissed her bruised lips, and they did it again.

It was wonderful.
It made her dizzy.
It set the pattern for the rest of her stay.

Kate enjoyed being an adulteress. She enjoyed walking around sore and swollen from intemperate lovemaking. She enjoyed spending much of her time in a lascivious daze. She also enjoyed a new-found confidence which led to her boldly initiating sex with Daniele. It happened on a Saturday morning while they were sharing the cramped bathroom after both had taken a shower. Daniele was bending over the sink attempting to retrieve the toothpaste cap that had fallen down the narrow plug-hole when she had a sudden impulse to slip her hand between his legs and grab him. His reaction to having his dangling parts manhandled while he was in such a vulnerable and – much worse – submissive position, was one of shock. So much so he was unable to get an erection until they had switched places and Kate was the one with her face pressed into the porcelain.

Kate did not tell Lidia about the affair with Pietro, of course, although she did complain about Daniele's domineering behaviour.

'He was a despot even in nappies,' Lidia agreed, as they sat side by side on the sofa sipping camomile tea. 'But it's my fault, too. I always treated him like a little king. Women of my generation didn't know any better, you see. We just did things the way they had always been done.'

There was no anxiety in her tone, no convulsions of guilt. What was past could not be changed and there was no point agonizing over it. Lidia was a wise woman. At peace with herself and the universe. She smiled sweetly at Kate, and the radiance of her Glorious Widowhood gave the comfortable room a golden glow.

Kate sighed. It was now seven-fifteen and two and a half hours had passed since she had come in from the garden. Sunlight still dappled the window-sill and a corner of the carpet but in contrast to that fondly remembered scene, Heather's living room seemed cheerless indeed. Prising herself off the sofa and into the bathroom, she peered again into the mirror over the sink. She was confronted by a woman staring contemptuously back at her. It was instant animosity.

'Lidia knows what's what,' the woman said with an insolent sneer. 'Passion troubles the spirit. Glorious Widowhood cannot be attained by anyone nurturing libidinous yearnings.'

Sons, Lovers, Etcetera

Kate watched the face darken with anger. 'Listen here!' she hissed, spraying the glass with outraged spittle. 'I might be vegetating. And I'm certainly hallucinating. But I'm not fucking nurturing anything at all!'

So get that straight, you bitch!

Chapter 7

As the days unfolded Heather, Maria and Lidia manifested so frequently it began to feel as though they had taken up residence. Indeed, the quality of their company was such that for much of the time Kate scarcely noticed she was alone. Heather and Maria, however, were concerned about her and disapproved of her solitary regime. In their opinion she slept too much, took too many baths and, as for talking to herself – well, it had simply got out of hand. Much to Kate's irritation they kept suggesting she do things, i.e. go swimming, take up aerobics, join an evening class, invite the podgy, sandy-haired bachelor who lived upstairs to join her in the garden for a neighbourly drink. But despite their nagging, it was Lena – on the one and only occasion she ever visited – who uttered the magic words that spurred her into taking action.

What she said was: 'If I've managed to survive all I've been through, then so can you.'

Anita had been Kate's twice-weekly home help for fourteen years. She arrived when Lorenzo was a thumb-sucking two-year-old and left when he was a posturing adolescent with Persol 649 sunglasses and an electric-blue Morini motor bike. She was the same age as Kate's mother and, like her mother, was afflicted with a restless and unfulfilled heart. The seeds of her suffering were sown when she became a domestic servant at the age of eleven and were nurtured daily by always wanting all that she did not have.

Her first job was with the family of a Fascist lawyer who worked her from six in the morning until eleven at night. She was fed kitchen scraps and her bed consisted of a two-foot-wide shelf above the wicker linen baskets lined up in the laundry room. Resentment at this treatment should have made a card-carrying Communist of her. Instead, everything about the family and their commodious apartment filled her with awe. The eight years spent waxing heavy wood furniture, polishing embossed silver and dusting with lingering devotion the perfume bottles on her mistress's mirrored dressing table, formed the woman she would become. Middle-class materialism became all that was desirable and soon replaced the Virgin Mary as her principal object of worship. And it was with the eldest son (a sneering youth whose gift on her fourteenth birthday was to pump her full of hot semen) that she had her first experience of love.

Cut her romantic teeth.
Or whatever you want to call it.

This painful and ultimately humiliating liaison set the pattern. From then on no bricklayer or car mechanic, no matter how handsome, ever stood a chance with her. Anita cooked and scrubbed and dropped her knickers exclusively for men who wore hand-tailored shirts and coaxed food particles from their teeth with ivory toothpicks. When she came to Kate she was by then a brisk spinster with coal-black eyes and a deep widow's peak, still dreaming of '*un signore*', a 'refined love', a 'prince among men' who would elevate her to the earthly paradise of a bourgeois marriage. Kate, who could not deny she was an impossible snob, adored her.

* * *

The action Anita spurred Kate into taking would not have met with her approval, however. She decided she would pay a visit to Luigi's, the Italian working-class café situated a couple of doors down from the corner shop where she bought her beans. The reason she wanted to go to Luigi's was because of the décor. Every time she passed, her eyes were drawn to Technicolor impressions of the Colosseum, a Venetian gondola and the Leaning Tower of Pisa with which an inspired brush had filled one wall. These electric images attracted her displaced spirit like a magnet. They put her in mind of day-trips to Ostia, making a pig of herself on pistachio ice-cream and of Signor Capellini in flat 8 singing '*O Sole Mio*' when he watered his geraniums. Another undoubted attraction was the gleaming Gaggia espresso machine.

The first time she went in she had a conversation with the grey-haired woman serving behind the red formica counter. The exchange lasted two minutes (quite a feat after so long talking only to herself), and went like this:

'*Buon giorno, signora. Un caffè, per favore.*'
'*Certo, signora. Italiana lei?*'
'*Si,*' Kate said, and at that moment it was no lie. '*Sono di Roma.*'
'*Ah, bella Roma.*'
'*Molto bella, si.*'

The coffee (the woman told her they used Lavazza) was black and bitter and Kate relished every drop. When she left she was about to say '*Arrivederci e grazie*', but the woman's head was turned away from her and she was staring out of the window. Kate did not need to be told that the tired eyes were blind to the traffic thundering along the Holloway Road. She knew as sure as she knew anything that they were fixed on the soaring peaks, dense pine forests and fragrant marigold fields of her lost Calabrian youth.

On her second visit a young man wearing little round spectacles and a green corduroy jacket sat at her table and tried to pick her up. 'Please don't think I'm rude,' he said pleasantly, 'but you've got such a nice face, I'd like to ask your advice on something. I'm thirty years old and I don't seem to have any luck with girls. Do you think I should join a dating agency?'

'I really can't say. I don't know anything about them.'

'I met a girl called Karen on a Club Med holiday in Greece last year. She seemed to like me until I told her what I do.'

'What do you do?'

'I'm an embalmer.'

'An embalmer? Of dead bodies?'

'Yes. Does that bother you?'

'Well . . . Not really, I suppose.'

'In that case, would you like to come out with me?'

'No, sorry.'

'I thought not. Well, never mind, it's been nice talking to you anyway.' He stood up and, with a gentle, philosophical smile, started for the door. As he did so Kate saw him stumble, lose his footing and disappear down a terrible vortex of his own.

The vortex!
The wandering pain!
At least, she said to herself, the coffee's good.

The third time Kate went to Luigi's an old classmate, and the person she had once envied more than anyone in the world, was there. In those days Sadie Harris (later Sadie Shaw), was a leggy blonde nymphette of breathtaking allure. She made the cover of *Nova* at seventeen, a

Hollywood film at eighteen and won the heart of a dreamboat pop star the year after that. While lesser mortals elbowed and clawed, Sadie was dropped into the welcoming arms of success like a prize-winning baby. It was not surprising, therefore (and had nothing to do with her unfocused state of mind) that Kate did not recognize the flushed and outsize matron with beefy arms and enormous breasts demolishing a gargantuan fry-up at the next table.

Fortunately Sadie's reaction to Kate's arrival made it clear that her own physiognomy had been spared such radical change.

'My God! It's Kate whatsit,' she exclaimed through a mouthful of egg and chips. 'Well, I never! Hey, wake up dum-dum – it's me, Sadie! Don't you remember?'

Above the fleshy neck the once beautiful face was like a bruised peach. Only the magnificence of the huge amber eyes was undiminished. Kate stared in disbelief. 'Sadie Harris?' she croaked. 'Goodness! I mean, well . . . how are you?'

'Fat, as you can see,' Sadie said. Then lumbering to her feet she transferred plate, roll and butter and mug of tea to Kate's table and, puffing like bellows, squeezed her bulk into the chair opposite. 'So? How long's it been? Fifteen years?'

'More like twenty.'

'Twenty? I don't believe it! Darling, have I got things to tell you!'

And she had.

The pink mouth opened wide and a great swollen river gushed forth, engulfing Kate with foam-crested breakers of bitterness and woe. It was a turbulent tale of Jealous Cows, Male Manipulators, Fame and Fortune Won and

Lost and Disappointment All Round. 'Didn't I hear you married a banker or something?' she interjected at one point in a vain attempt to divert the flow and save herself from drowning.

'Don?' Sadie shrieked and everybody in the café turned round. 'Don't mention that name! We're divorced now, thank Christ, but just because I got the house he thinks he's done all right by me. What do I care about ten fucking rooms anyway? Jasmine's away at boarding school and the dog died last week. Since the poor little bugger's gone I rattle around the place like a loose nail in a shoebox. My ex doesn't give two shits, of course, but what can you expect? All men are bastards. The one I've got now is twenty-four going on fourteen and skinny as a stick insect, with acne. Bounces my tits around like beanbags and thinks he's a great lover. Piss on him is what I say.'

The mouth trembled. Strangled sounds gurgled deep in the gullied recesses of her throat. Mascara dissolved and traced sooty pathways over undulating hills and valleys to the dimple in her fleshy chin. Kate watched the progress of those grim, wandering tracks with an aching compassion. To her they were nothing less than the universal hieroglyphics of womankind's grief. And fumbling for a screwed-up tissue in her jeans pocket, she wept too.

It was early afternoon when they left the café. The sky had clouded over, there was a frisky wind and it had started to rain. 'Well, goodbye,' Kate said, shivering a little in her T-shirt. 'We really must try to meet . . .'

But Sadie was not yet ready for the austerity of her lonely mansion. 'Fuck that,' she interrupted impatiently. 'I've got a bottle of brandy in my bag – Italian stuff, Vecchia something or other. I'm coming back with you.'

Which she did, collapsing on Heather's sofa the

moment they got through the door. A couple of snifters later, however, she was revived and cheerful, exercising her lungs with a medley of nostalgic favourites from their rock 'n' roll youth. It took that bit longer for the alcohol to reach Kate's singing voice but when it did, she chorused along with her. They did 'Satisfaction', 'Can't Buy Me Love', 'Yellow Submarine', 'The Sounds of Silence', 'Heartbreak Hotel', 'Eleanor Rigby' and many more. At eight o'clock Kate served beans on toast and at nine-thirty Sadie called a taxi and heaved off home. Five minutes later the phone rang. It was Lorenzo.

At the time of the Louisa business and Kate's subsequent departure, Lorenzo was holidaying on the island of Ponza with his girlfriend. Too distraught to handle a phone call, Kate instead sent a brief note explaining that he 'wasn't to worry', but she was going to London 'to sort a few things out'. As it happened Lorenzo's life at that moment was particularly gratifying and he found it impossible to worry about anything or anyone. He was young, in love and his only concerns for the next couple of months would be eating, sleeping, swimming, sunbathing, smoking dope and making love (although not necessarily in that order). Every day Kate's enveloping arms were less constraining. Every day her controlling voice rang fainter in his ears. Every day he felt himself more of a man.

In other words, it was all right for some.

The reason he was phoning now was because his father was making a fuss at having to look after himself. As Lidia refused to have him on any permanent basis, Daniele was insisting that (until such time as Kate recovered her senses) Lorenzo do his filial duty and return to the nest. Lorenzo, more than comfortable with his girlfriend, was horrified.

'*Non è giusto! Lui* can't dictate to me like he did to you,' he protested to Kate in muddled Italish. 'No way he can expect me to *occupare le tue* shoes.'

Kate felt his breath hot and anxious in her ear. She saw the nervous tugging of his earlobe, his green-flecked eyes widening for emphasis, the unkempt tangle of his sun-bleached hair. '*Lui vuole* that I do the cooking! I mean, I've got exams to prepare,' he continued, his voice rising to an outraged whine. 'Dad's putting the guilt screws on me and it's just not fair.'

Sweetest darling, her heart cried. My only love! Treasure of my life!

Fortunately, however, she managed to keep these maternal ravings to herself. 'You're a big boy now, Lorenzino,' was all she said. 'Tell him it's out of the question and stand firm.'

Later as she lay sleepless in bed Sister Luigina rustled down echoing marble corridors to be at her side. The long face was even more sorrowful and the grey whiskers seemed to spring with increased vigour from the sharp chin. 'What is it, my child?' she asked, leaning over and taking her hand. 'That same silly old pain?'

Kate nodded, but her tongue lay stiff and dry against her palate and she could not speak. 'My pain,' she wanted to tell her, 'is more than a pain. It's a corrosive acid consuming me from the inside. It has taken my kidneys, liver, stomach, lungs and heart. I'm as hollow as a kettledrum. At night a phantom heartbeat gallops through the empty chambers of my five-six frame. Soon I will collapse in on myself. My bones will crumble and my skin will flake. This pain is my funeral pyre. In the morning all you will find is a handful of dust.'

Chapter 8

Before Kate started going to Luigi's café the only place she came into contact with her fellows was the Cleanwash washeteria; an establishment sandwiched between a shoe shop specializing in vertiginously spiked footwear for big-footed transvestites and a Perfect Chicken take-away. She went once a week – always on a washday Monday – and she always looked forward to the visits.

Objectively speaking, it was neither an inviting nor uplifting place. The decorative theme was blue and yellow. There was a false ceiling constructed from yellow board panels (many of which were partially dislodged, splintered or trailing curls of disconnected wire), walls lined with mosaic-effect blue plastic and a long blue bench with chrome edging that faced a barrage of bilious yellow washing-machines. The five huge driers situated at the back were also bilious yellow, and bilious yellow predominated among the blacks, browns and greys of the flecked (and usually litter-strewn) Granno floor. Even the poster advertising the detergents available from the Soap Shop dispenser was unintentionally colour-coordinated. Cheerily urging customers to 'Wash in that summertime feeling', it showed a shapely female with drifting mermaid hair gliding through water of a deep, Mediterranean blue. Or, as the manufacturers would probably say:

A Bold blue.

Vida Adamoli

An Ariel blue.
A fabulous Fairy blue.

For Kate, doing her dirty washing in public (so to speak) was a new experience. The concept, however, was a familiar one. After all, Cleanwash was nothing other than a mechanized plastic fount. A modern-day equivalent to the fizzing fresh water streams where women throughout the ages had gathered to sing, gossip and beat their linen on stones made round and smooth by successive generations of labouring hands. Even Lidia, brought up in a small coastal village south of Rome, remembered the camaraderie of collective laundering before the port was built and the deep gully of limpid water that served as the community basin was drained and filled in.

Cleanwash, of course, was a different time and a different place. Instead of the slap, slap, slap of clothes smacking against boulders, the launderette reverberated with the rhythmic chugging of revolving drums, punctuated by frisky snaps and clicks of buttons and zips hitting metal and glass. In lieu of lacy clusters of soap, bubbles embroidering the surface of icy eddies, detergent foam flopped, slopped and slavered like idiot spittle down porthole windows. And needless to say, no sun pressed between the shoulder-blades of toiling backs. There was only the formidable blast of dry, scorched air that seared Kate's nostrils every time she opened her drier to retrieve its incandescent contents – not something many would enjoy but which gave her a powerful olfactory buzz. In Lidia's opinion, this furtive pleasure did not indicate that Kate was a solvent-sniffer in the making. It was simply a sensory compensation for emotional, physical and spiritual deprivation and probably wouldn't last.

Which Kate found very reassuring.

Sons, Lovers, Etcetera

* * *

That said, emotional, physical and spiritual deprivation most certainly contributed to the hungry interest she took in other Cleanwash patrons. She was fascinated by the assortment of items produced from bulging rucksacks, holdalls and leatherette shopping trolleys, as well as the individual stamp people imposed on their set routines. The contained triumph with which they commandeered a favourite machine, for example, or the manner in which bedlinen, towels and personal attire was caressed or casually manhandled. In Italy, undisguised interest in the business of others is commonplace and offends few. Not so in Britain. In deference to native sensibility, therefore, Kate resorted to peeking, peering and sly sidelong glances. And if anyone sensed her stealthy gaze they gave no indication of it. Seemingly oblivious to any intrusion, they perused papers and magazines, chatted to companions or stared raptly at their churning belongings trapped behind the automaton's Cyclopean eye.

On one occasion she did get caught out. On that day the object of her scrutiny was a tall, attractive black woman wearing a black PVC baseball hat, silver hoop earrings and skin-tight leggings. Kate was captivated both by the vast amount of washing she was doing (for which she needed all four of the larger capacity machines), as well as by her backside. This detail of her anatomy was so remarkable it would mesmerize anyone. Not only was it extremely large, it was also wondrously firm and perfectly spherical. In fact, it looked exactly like a gardener's dream of a prize-winning tomato.

But for Kate the present was a slippery reality. She was constantly falling through trapdoors and ending up somewhere else.

* * *

Vida Adamoli

In this instance the trapdoor was the woman's backside. One minute she was in the launderette, the next back with Daniele, reliving his admiration for the *pomodoro*-shaped bottom (which she did not possess) and, more specifically, his lecherous attentions to a certain Elizabeth (who did). The effect of this unwelcome recollection was to resurrect sour and resentful feelings, disturbing the wounded lion that dwelt in her heart. And deafened by its outraged roar she let her guard drop. Distracted and abstracted she openly – and rudely – stared.

Fortunately Lorna (as the woman later introduced herself) was not offended. She interpreted Kate's interest as admiration for the purple dress she had taken from the machine and was now carefully examining.

'Looks OK, doesn't it?' she said, holding the garment up and giving it a vigorous shake. 'I'd have been really miffed if it'd shrunk or anything. I'm not so sure about these creases, though. They'll be a bugger to iron out,' she paused to fiddle with the frilled neck, adding, 'I like purple, don't you?'

Kate was not merely embarrassed at having her interest noticed, she was mortified (almost as mortified as when she was caught cheating in a spelling test aged nine).

'Yes,' she gulped – and getting that word out was like prising a stuck cork from a bottle – continuing in a rush, 'I had a purple dress once. But it was plain, without the frills. And I couldn't wash it, either. It had to be drycleaned.'

Lorna laughed. 'I never take no notice of labels. As I always say, anything can be washed as long as you do it right.'

Lorna had plenty of advice about 'doing it right', which covered right soap powder, right fabric conditioner, right temperature and right programme. Like Kate's mother she also subscribed to the maxim that cleanliness is next to godliness, a possible explanation as to why she was undertaking such a formidable load. She was so relaxed and friendly, so delightfully chatty, that Kate quickly recovered her composure and offered to help with the folding of a king-size duvet cover.

'You don't mind?'

'Of course not.'

'Well, thanks, hon. You're an angel!'

What followed was the best half-hour Kate had spent in ages. Once the duvet cover was done, she and Lorna went on to tackle all the larger items. As they worked (their movements smoothly synchronized as though they'd folded washing together dozens of times before) Lorna related the details of where she had bought things and exactly how much they cost. She also told her the story of a neatly mended tear that went down the centre of a cotton coverlet.

'See that? It was done by the big toenail of this guy I was having a thing with,' she said, lowering her voice confidentially. 'You just wouldn't believe the great horny ridges that man had on his feet. Talons they were. "Bring a chain saw," I used to say, "and I'll give you a pedicure."'

They giggled. Lorna's white teeth flashed and the silver hoop earrings danced against her cheeks. As she was admiring her Kate realized she was feeling almost happy. They had made a real connection, of that she was sure, and there was even the chance they might become friends. She savoured this possibility throughout the week and returned to Cleanwash full of hope that Lorna would reappear (this time she planned to further their intimacy by sharing *her* washing tips). But Lorna did not show up that Monday, nor the one after. In fact, they never did meet again – although for weeks afterwards Kate continued to keep an eye out for her. Eventually she accepted that theirs was destined to be a brief encounter.

Ships passing in the night, etcetera, etcetera.

After Lorna, there was a new element to Kate's interest in Cleanwash customers. She was on the lookout for another warm and communicative soul with whom she might form an acquaintance. The next person she got into conversation with, however, was neither warm nor communicative – at least not initially. He was a mean-looking skinhead with barbed wire tattooed around his left bicep and a definitely hostile aura. That day a sudden storm had emptied the streets and, with the exception of a girl in her early teens who sat in a morose lump chain-smoking, they were the only ones using the launderette. Which meant that when the lather in his machine – the next but one from hers – began turning pink she was obliged to draw his attention to it. (Years of domesticity had programmed her to respond to anyone's laundry crisis.)

'Excuse me,' she stretched out a tentative hand and tapped his arm. 'But it looks like you've got something running in there.'

'Wot?' the skinhead said vacantly (the reason he had not spotted this for himself was because he was absorbed in scraping dirt from under his fingernails with the tip of a penknife). Then he saw what she was on about. With a desperate howl he lunged forward and slammed his fist against the glass. 'I don't believe it! My new 501s!' He swung round and glared ferociously at her. 'It's them fuckin' red socks!'

Kate recoiled instinctively. But her fear evaporated when she saw the tears welling up in his eyes. Considering the real tragedies of life, a display of grief over ruined jeans is not something most people would respond to with sympathy. But Kate had been through the same experience with Lorenzo. Twice. On the first occasion the culprit was a Made in Taiwan T-shirt. The second, coincidentally, a pair of socks. And on both occasions it was the ruin of beloved jeans that had provoked tears.

'Don't worry,' she said soothingly. 'All's not lost. This is what you've got to do . . .'

She went on to describe Lena's method of salvage (a tip she had anticipated sharing with Lorna) which involved repeatedly dunking the item in boiling bleach until the rogue dye was washed out and the original colour restored.

'But they'll end up bleedin' *white*!'

'Well, they'll fade a bit,' Kate conceded. 'But not much. You'll hardly notice the difference. The important thing is to rinse them thoroughly in plenty of cold water.'

The young man slumped back on the bench and stared thoughtfully at his Doc Martens. 'I'll get Stan to do it. He'll grovel at the chance.' Kate looked puzzled, so he explained. 'Stan's a tosser. He's one of my slaves.'

Which was how the subject of sado-masochism came up.

The skinhead was short and scrawny with a neck as thin and vulnerable as a glabrous fledgling. That he also nurtured the tenderest of emotions was eloquently demonstrated by the concern he had for his clothes. Despite these handicaps – or so they seemed to Kate – he proceeded to inform her that he was a respected 'master' on the gay S&M scene. Details he gave included the gear he wore (leather, chains, military caps, German jackboots), the nature of the tasks he imposed and the fact that he had run up a £650 bill on an S&M sex phone line. The size of this sum pleased him, despite not being able to pay the bill and having now had his phone cut off. For some odd reason he regarded this as confirmation of his power and status.

Part of his reason for telling Kate all this was to boast. But he also wanted to express gratitude for her kindly concern.

'One good turn deserves another,' he declared earnestly. 'You've helped me so I'll help you. What do you want? Floors scrubbed? Ironing? Windows cleaned? The garden dug? One word from me and my minions will be knocking on your door in minutes.'

This was an unexpected and tempting offer. Kate's thoughts lingered briefly on the rubbery build-up of grease and dirt she had avoided investigating behind the cooker. There was also a door that needed rehanging, the dripping tap in the bathroom, several loose floorboards, peeling lino, shelves to . . . She stopped the list there. As she reminded herself, there were some things she couldn't and wouldn't consider. Besides which, she was not convinced he could really deliver. After all, why was a slave-master doing his own washing?

'That's very kind,' she said, making the excuse that she was staying with a friend who liked to do everything herself.

'You sure?'

'Really.'

For a moment he seemed disappointed, and then his attention reverted to the problem at hand. He pulled the pink-tinged jeans out of the machine, gazed at them sorrowfully, then stuffed them into a rucksack along with the rest of his ruined wash. Then, with a casual 'See you around', he strode manfully out of the launderette. It had been a bizarre encounter but Kate had enjoyed it.

In fact, she was sorry to see him go.
(Too much solitude and anyone can seem endearing.)

By then the storm was over and the rain had stopped.

Cars speeding along the waterlogged road outside made sharp swishing sounds as though they were tearing through silk. The teenage girl was still there, staring gloomily out of the window and kicking at the squashed dog-ends that had proliferated around her feet. Kate dumped her washing into a plastic basket and carried it over to the driers. As she was doing so the door was flung open and a grim-faced woman of about her own age with hunched shoulders and grim-set lips burst in. She marched straight over to the girl and whacked her so hard around the head Kate felt her own spinning.

'Ouch!' the screech was ear-splitting. 'What's that for? I haven't done nothing!'

'You deceitful little brat!'

'I don't know what you're on about!'

'Oh, so you don't know what I'm on about?' The woman took another swipe, but this time the girl was ready and ducked out of reach.

'Leave off! I told you, I haven't done nothing!'

'Say that again and I'll bloody kill you! I've found it – stuffed inside your swimming bag. You've really done it this time, young lady. You're in for it now and no mistake!'

At this the girl began to snivel. 'It wasn't my fault. Sharon was the one who—'

But the woman was having none of it. 'Clear off!' she screamed. 'I'll deal with you at home!'

Keeping a wide berth the girl dived for the door and skedaddled. The woman yanked the machine open and began ferociously tugging at its contents. She did so with such force that the twisted tangle of flower-sprigged sheets sailed clear of the basket and landed smack on the grubby floor.

'Damn,' she muttered. Then she tipped the wet mound back into the machine, fished three pound coins out of her purse and pressed the On button. There was a brief pause, then the drum gave a lurch and the carousel started up again.

'Kids!' she said, glancing briefly at Kate and sighing. It was a sound sucked from the great reservoir of female exasperation. 'What a nightmare! If we knew the worst no one would bother to have 'em.'

Kate, of course – standing by the drier with nose hairs quivering in anticipation of the hot blast they'd get when she opened the door – knew what the woman had yet to find out. Which was that once a child has flown the nest, a mother becomes nostalgic for even the most evil behaviour. Now wasn't the moment for truth, however, but for solidarity.

'You're right,' she said.

And her smile hid her lie and her loneliness.

Chapter 9

Kate felt a sympathetic bond with anyone trying to cope with adolescents. She had evolved her own theory as to the purpose this period in human development served. It came to her in a moment of inspired clarity after Lorenzo, aged thirteen, stormed out of the flat after she refused to tolerate 'Born in the USA' playing full blast. By that time she was becoming used to loutish and defiant behaviour. It had started around twelve and went with the poisonously smelly feet, the endless telling of cretinous jokes and chortling pleasure he derived from igniting farts (on one occasion actually burning a hole in his pyjama trousers).

'Forget everything you've read or heard,' she told Maria one afternoon as they sunned themselves among pots of lemon-scented geraniums on Kate's terrace. 'The function of adolescence has nothing to do with a child's psychological growth. It is simply an expression of Mother Nature's compassionate desire to protect the poor mother. I mean, think about it. If it wasn't for the transformation of her perfect angel into an acned churl, how could she survive the pain when he eventually upped and left her? The answer, of course, is she couldn't. She would curl up and die from grief.'

It was a hot Roman day in mid-May. In the street below women were clustering around a lorry selling peaches the size of small melons for 3,000 lire a kilo. Maria, sprawled inelegantly on a Lilo, was angling Fulvio's shaving mirror so that it bounced tanning rays on to the most intimate region of her inner thighs.

'You're so right,' she agreed with injured conviction. 'But I didn't have to wait for adolescence to know Lina was destined to be a mega pain in the bum. I knew it from the moment she was put into my arms and I got my first look at her.'

Lina (off school because of supposedly crippling period pains) was eavesdropping on this conversation from their balcony immediately below. With one hand she pressed a tepid hot-water bottle to her stomach, with the other she smoked a filched Marlboro. Initially she was only half listening, her attention focused on practising sophisticated and seductive inhaling and exhaling techniques. On hearing herself described as a 'mega pain in the bum', however, she became all ears.

Lina was not a physically appealing teenager. She was small and thin like her father and had inherited his sallow complexion and large, beaky nose. At the point of her mother's unforgivable utterance her eyes narrowed, her top lip curled to reveal long front teeth and her face took on the expression of an outraged rodent. After which she stubbed out the cigarette, stuck her fingers down her throat and regurgitated the spaghetti she had eaten for lunch all over the cream upholstery of Maria's new sunbed.

Barf!

Eight years later Kate found herself expounding her theory all over again. This time it was to explain to Sadie why her daughter (briefly home before departing with her father for a Caribbean holiday) could call her, among other things, a 'disgusting and hateful witch'. As it happened Sadie was more angry than upset. Jasmine was not a consuming passion and never had been. In fact, she charted the start of her decline from the fateful night Don screwed her in the back of his Rolls and conception took place.

'I started piling on the weight seconds after he ejaculated,' she declared resentfully. 'The message going out to all my neurons was *Pile on the lard!* In nine months I went from eight-five to thirteen stone. I was twenty-six and I had three chins, four stomachs, haemorrhoids and varicose veins. Don said the more of me the better and shovelled champagne and hand-made chocolates down my throat. What a shit! When Jasmine was six weeks old I walked into the nursery and there he was, screwing the anorexic Norland nanny.'

Hearing this made Kate sit bolt upright. 'I don't believe it!' she exclaimed. 'When I was twenty-six I found my husband screwing a Norland nanny, too!'

Which might seem too much of a coincidence, but it was absolutely true.

Daniele's Norland nanny came into their lives when Marco Rossi, Daniele's friend and colleague on the newspaper, brought her over from England to take charge of his three-year-old twins. This was not his idea (his wage was average and his views left-wing), but his wife's. The daughter of a rich and influential industrialist, Elena had embarked on married life determined to live happily with whatever her husband's income provided. It was only a matter of months, however, before the financial rigours of being Signora Rossi had her teetering on the edge of a breakdown. At which point her father stepped in and their one-bedroomed flat in Trastevere was exchanged for a villa with live-in servants on the Appia Antica. Kate was delighted at the move. As she used to say to Daniele, it made more of an occasion when they were invited for dinner.

The day they met Caroline, Elena had organized a lunch party in the ornate gazebo that sheltered under spreading elms at the edge of the lawn. Caroline was a strapping blonde with a round, freckled face from Calderdale in West Yorkshire, and everybody agreed she looked most adorable in her trademark brown uniform.

'The trouble is she's never been abroad before and she's miserably homesick,' Elena confided, leading Kate over to the children's table where Caroline was feeding her charges pizza slices and ice-cream. 'Be a darling and see if you can cheer her up for me. Talk to her about England.'

Which Kate very kindly did. They discussed the royal family (Caroline was a staunch royalist) and *Coronation Street* (how hard it was to live without it). Caroline also divulged her secret for a perfect rice pudding: a splashing of orange flower water and plenty of double cream. After a while they were joined by Daniele, well watered and in one of his expansive and complimentary moods.

'Give Rome a chance and it will know how to welcome you,' he told her with a roguish grin. 'After all, when has the Eternal City ever let a pretty girl down?'

Caroline was charmed. So charmed, in fact, that she abandoned her customary reserve and asked if she might visit on her Sunday off. The first time she came Kate served home-made scones and they all played Scrabble. The second time it was home-made fruit cake and they played Monopoly. The third time she stayed for supper, after which Lidia arrived to babysit and Kate and Daniele took Caroline to Judy Kendall's thirtieth birthday party.

Judy, an entomologist specializing in the study of mosquitoes, worked for the UN Food and Agricultural Organization. Normally a cheerful and high-spirited girl, she had been dumped that very evening by her boyfriend (he phoned as she was zipping herself into a sexy black number to inform her he was madly in love with someone else). As a consequence Kate was commandeered on arrival to join three others endeavouring to give sisterly support to the distraught woman weeping, ranting and banging her head in the bedroom. Around midnight, anaesthetized by a litre or two of recklessly swigged Frascati, Judy collapsed on the bed and within seconds was snoring. By which time Kate had lost any festive urge. It was time, she decided, to go home.

The apartment was high-ceilinged, spacious and teeming with guests. Elbowing her way through the crush Kate set off in search of Daniele and Caroline. She searched the living room, dining room, kitchen and the large terrace where people were boogying under a clear and starry sky. Eventually she looked in the boxroom where Judy kept glass cases of mounted insects and her camping equipment. And it was there – on a pile of folded groundsheets – that she found them.

'Don't tell me!' Sadie shrieked, tossing her head in outrage and contemptuous disgust. 'She had her tits hanging out, his trousers were falling off his hairy arse and they were going at it like a pair of snorting heifers!'

Exactly.

This conversation on adolescence, Norland nannies, and so on, was conducted on Heather's minuscule patch of lawn. It was an overcast day with a snappish wind but Sadie pronounced herself too 'freaked out' to stay inside. She had turned up late morning looking like a giant jelly baby wearing a bubble-gum pink track suit with her blonde hair sprouting from several ribboned bunches on top of her head. (The bandaged hand was the result of lashing out at Jasmine and hitting the edge of a marble coffee table instead.)

Before calling on Kate, Sadie had spent a period of reflection in the Brompton Oratory. She was a regular visitor to this church – not because she was a Catholic (by her own definition she was nothing), nor was it because she was drawn to the candles and sumptuously ornate decoration. The reason was that it was there she experienced her one and only miracle.

'It was the day my divorce became absolute and I finally tipped the scales at fifteen stone,' she told Kate. 'I'd abandoned myself to total despair when suddenly the Virgin, before whom I was seated, raised a plaster finger and made a distinct prodding movement to my left. I turned my head to see what she was pointing at and, lo and behold, a golden-haired youth in a red anorak appeared from behind a pillar and winked at me. At that moment the cloud lifted. I knew I'd been sent a sign that life was still worth living. But I don't expect you to believe me. After all, nobody else does.'

As it so happened Kate did believe her. During her twenty years in Rome she had heard many testimonies of this sort. Lidia herself told the story of praying to the Madonna on the morning of her wedding and looking up to see a shimmering tear ooze out of the painted blue eye. If only, she would say sighing and shaking her head, she'd had sense enough to heed the warning. It was the divine encounters of Signor Conti, however – unhinged since the day his wife walked out taking their two children with her – which impressed Kate the most. They were so wonderfully humdrum and domestic.

As he told everyone who would listen, 'The Day Rosalba left me, Jesus Christ moved in.'

From the very start Signor Conti's relationship with his exalted cohabitant proved as difficult and fractious as the one he'd had with his wife. If anything they actually quarrelled more because Rosalba had ways of shutting him up that the Man from Nazareth clearly never mastered. On one occasion Kate returned home from the market to find her neighbour standing in his garden berating the pear tree.

'Don't try and tell me you died on the cross,' he shouted, spraying spittle and shaking his fist. 'You were never put on the cross in the first place. You and I know full well what killed you. It was varicose veins!'

'Cigarette?' Sadie asked, offering her packet.

'Thanks.'

They lit up at the same time as somebody a few doors down put on Mahler's Symphony No. 5 at top volume. Then Mad Max appeared on the wall where earlier in the summer an army of aphids had feasted on Heather's honeysuckle. Watching the tendrils of smoke curling from her fingers, Kate let her mind go on another drift. She saw herself once again, five months pregnant, feeding sardines to the seals at the Villa Borghese zoo. The sardines, five silver slithers wrapped in thick brown paper, cost 200 lire from the whiskery matriarch who ran the kiosk near by.

'Don't give Mussolini any,' she said, handing Kate the parcel. 'He's a bully and too greedy for his own good.'

The old bull was indeed a tyrant, a strutting, posturing heavyweight who lorded it over the three females who shared his pool. When he went for a swim his great muscular body cut the water like a seven-foot torpedo, ruthlessly butting all obstacles out of his way. But it was as a scrounger that he excelled. Heaving his wriggling bulk forward to the railings, he reared up on his stiffly splayed flippers and barked roaring commands to be fed.

Although she would never had admitted it to anyone, Kate found Mussolini's macho presence thrilling. His fierce concentration of purpose enthralled her. The sinuous power and rippled silkiness of his quivering torso mesmerized her in an almost sexual way. To atone for this she always did her best to make sure the females got their share, tossing the fish high over his head or too far to the side for him to chase. The last fish, however, was reserved for him. On this occasion the old bull plucked it deftly from the air, swallowed it on one gulp, then turned slowly to stare at her.

'It was as though I was being sucked into another dimension, taken to the watery world of my primitive origins,' she said to Sadie, hesitating over the words as she tried to explain. 'For a brief moment I floated in amniotic fluid like the foetus I was carrying in my womb. And in that fleeting space of time I instinctively understood the connection between all life forms in the universe.'

Sadie (not surprisingly) was impressed.

'Really?' she said, wonderingly, her huge amber eyes shining like golden nuggets in aspic.

'Yes,' said Kate. 'Really.'

Chapter 10

Before she left, Sadie told Kate that her 'horrible child' was in love (she knew this from overhearing Jasmine wax lyrical about a puerile stud called Masher). Kate who had yet to meet the girl, was not exactly riveted by the news. Nevertheless, she simulated interest, offering a few reflections, admittedly hackneyed, on the affecting and tender nature of young love. Sadie interrupted her with an impatient snort.

'Come off it,' she snapped. 'You know as well as I do there's a big fat worm in that pretty apple. The only question is, how long will it take her to find it?'

She was right, of course. Kate's own first love – lean, mean and fifteen – had stolen her heart with romantic declarations and long, steamy, above-the-waist petting sessions. When repeated attempts to storm her knicker elastic failed, however, he blithely transferred his affections to Janet Hart.

'But he said he loved me,' she sobbed bitterly to her mother.

To which her mother replied sadly, 'They usually do, darling. They usually do.'

Which was pretty cryptic and did not help Kate one iota.

Kate's gift to Lorenzo's sexual awakening was to be

everything her own mother was not. That is to say she was reassuring, sympathetic and informative. She saw herself as a sort of maternal Virgil, holding a steady lamp to guide him through the *Inferno* of hormonal confusion and anarchy. The fact that she was besieged with anxieties, however, often made it hard to fulfil this role. For the most part these anxieties were the same as any parents'. That is to say, heartbreak, Aids and all the other sexually transmitted diseases. But she also gave herself an extra worry: premature ejaculation.

Maria, usually a source of encouragement and cheer, was responsible for this. During one hot, slobbed-out afternoon, wearing an old vest of Fulvio's stretched tight over her swinging breasts and bare, quivering thighs, she told Kate about her brother-in-law (the one who painted nudes and worked for a bank). It was a tragic tale of thrills and spills and, in a nutshell, went like this:

Pino, in common with many Italian males, lost his virginity to a married woman – in this instance the forty-five-year-old aunt of his best friend. The seduction began when she surreptitiously fondled his thigh during a meal celebrating the friend's successful exam results, and concluded six months later the week he turned sixteen.

The event took place in her living room while her husband was out at a football match (Lazio beat Catanzaro 3-0) and her daughter was at the orthodontist having her brace readjusted. It was the first time in all the months of intense build-up that they had been alone together and they lunged at each other even before the front door was properly closed. Mouths locked, hands groped and tongues wrestled with the ferocity of sea lions battling it out during the mating season. After about four and a half minutes, however, this all became too much. The aunt flung herself on the chintz-covered sofa and, with an animal cry, begged her young stud to take her.

At which point Pino's knees buckled and his eyeballs rolled back in his head. He pitched forward and with a helpless moan sunk like a stone between her invitingly splayed legs. Semen (an eggcupfull at the very least!) seeped shamefully through his chinos leaving a damp and sticky stain. The kid hadn't even managed to unzip his trousers.

'Poor thing,' murmured Kate, distressed. 'He must have been traumatized.'

'He was,' Maria replied sombrely. 'But the worst is he's never recovered. My sister says that in fifteen years of marriage he's only managed to do it three times.'

At the time of this conversation Lorenzo still had a good two years before puberty. But a subversive seed of disquiet had been planted and Kate was destined to nurture it.

And Lorenzo, bless him, to endure the consequences.

She first broached the subject when he confessed being attracted to a girl he had spent the whole of elementary school disliking – he was more than anything puzzled by this given she had tree-trunk legs, a moustache and in no way conformed to his physical ideal (at that time a cross between Tinkerbell and Madonna). From then on she returned to it with obsessive insistence whenever she suspected he had a new female interest. The message she was so determined to drive home was actually level-headed and reassuring: i.e. that it was common for sexually inexperienced boys to suffer premature ejaculation and on no account was he to feel a failure if it happened to him. The moment she started on about it, however, he dismissed her with a bored 'I know, you keep telling me', and disappeared.

The fact was Lorenzo had his own worries regarding his Big Moment, which, sensibly deciding it was his business not hers, he kept to himself. The main problem was confusing the two entry options and taking the wrong way in. He was also bothered by advice given to him by the delivery boy from their local grocery shop.

'It all boils down to rhythm,' the youth said, with an authoritative, snaggle-toothed leer. 'Get that right and you've got the whole thing sussed.'

Lorenzo repeated this cryptic utterance to a couple of schoolmates and soon it was doing the rounds. No one was prepared to admit they hadn't a clue what it mean, of course.

When the time came, however, at a beach party with a girl he'd only known a few days, everything went like a dream. After some unavoidable fumbling to start with, he soon familiarized himself with the mysteries of her intimate anatomy and worked out what was what. Penetration followed almost immediately, after which the bit was between his teeth and the 'rhythm thing' took care of itself. As for premature ejaculation, he was able to reassure Kate on that count.

'No problem,' he told her nonchalantly. 'I concentrated on reciting *Ave Maria* in my head. And it worked.'

Kate's relief that Lorenzo had escaped Pino's fate was profound. And although his delaying tactic was one she hoped he would soon be able to dispense with, she was proud he had been so enterprising. Apart from anything else, the boy hadn't even been brought up a Catholic!

For Lorenzo losing his virginity was a triumph he boasted loudly about to all and sundry. Falling in love, however, which happened less than three weeks later, was a starry-eyed joy of dizzying intensity which instinct told him not to share – he did not fancy being teased by his friends, and, most of all, he wanted to avoid the interference of his mother. Needless to say he had no luck there.

Maternal instinct – the only thing Kate trusted implicitly – alerted her within days. There was the moony abstraction, the lack of interest in things that had previously been priorities, the endless phone conversations conducted *sotto voce* from her bedroom extension. He also developed an obsessive preoccupation with his appearance, especially his hair. Most telling of all, however, was his emotional withdrawal. It was quite clear that everything significant, all meaning and purpose, was now exclusively focused on the private enchantment of two.

Up until then Kate had always found jealousy, though unpleasant, pretty straightforward. It was the expected response to sexual or emotional betrayal, or wanting what someone else had got. Where Lorenzo was concerned things got muddled. Her desire for his happiness was constantly tripping over resentment at being demoted in his affections. Consequently, it took a while before she recognized what she was dealing with. Once she did, however, it did not require long sessions of in-depth self-analysis to realize her rival was not Paoletta (who was pretty, well-mannered and, like Lorenzo, fourteen and a half) but simply life itself. For the reality was that her Darling Boy, her Be All and End All, was outgrowing the things that she could provide.

Her glory days were over.
The countdown had started.
His phantom bags stood packed and ready by the door.

Unceremoniously – and with unbecoming haste – the ghost of his future had arrived and was squatting on her present.

Vida Adamoli

* * *

At the same moment as Kate was awakening to this painful truth, Lorenzo and Paoletta were having their photograph taken at a studio which provided costumes for clients to dress up in. Paoletta, in a satin dress with a high, lace-trimmed neck, tight pleated bodice and flouncy skirt, was a Southern belle. Her big dark eyes peeped appealingly from under a picture hat festooned with ribbons and she carried a fancy parasol. Lorenzo, proud and manly in his Confederate uniform, had armed himself with an impressive sword and scabbard, as well as a hefty rifle.

They returned the next day to collect two copies of the result. The woman in reception presented them with a sepia-toned vision of unparalleled perfection, tastefully mounted on brown card with a curlicue pattern in gold around the border.

'Like it?' she smiled.

Awe robbed them of speech. All they could do was nod.

When Lorenzo returned home his face was shining with happiness. It was their 'marriage photo', he explained, sliding it carefully out of its protective envelope to show Kate. The sacred commemoration of their eternal love.

This happened at just gone four. At five Kate was walking past shuttered kiosks in the tree-lined market street where Lidia lived. She arrived at the calm and sun-dappled flat just as a bridge game finished and the clique of merry widows was leaving (an empty Campari bottle and the generous scattering of macaroon crumbs on the table testifying to the delightfully indulgent time had by all). Lidia welcomed her with a kiss and a hug, followed by a shrewdly appraising glance that took in all. Then she produced a second bottle of Campari and poured them both a glass.

'So, *cara*,' she said, urging Kate into her deceased

husband's comfortable chair. 'Tell me. What's that son of mine done this time?'

'Not your son, mine,' Kate sighed, lighting a cigarette and taking a swig from her glass (in that order). 'I mean, it's not that he's running riot or anything like that, but he just doesn't live on this planet any more. If he isn't sleeping or on the phone, then he's walking around with his head in the clouds. I can't get him to do anything. I talk myself blue in the face but nothing goes in. Take today, for instance. We'd agreed to go to the Rinascente to buy a new mattress for his bed. I even reminded him about it at breakfast. Then what does he do?' And with hurt trembling at the edge of her voice she told Lidia about the photograph business.

Lidia knew at once that Kate was not upset because her shopping plans had been disrupted. 'You have to accept that Lorenzino's growing up,' she said gently. 'He's a big boy now.'

'Not too big to fall flat on his face, though. He worries me and he exasperates me. He's just so full of romantic dreams.'

'Ah, romantic dreams! Let the dear child enjoy them while they last,' Lidia's expression was tender, and as she spoke her blue-veined old hands fluttered like wounded butterflies. 'Sooner or later the day will come when he finds they've all disappeared. Like footsteps in melting snow. Like dust scattering before the wind.'

While Kate's ears were tuned to the echo of these distant words, the overcast sky turned ominously leaden and Sadie's complaints became a muffled, background rumble. A few minutes later, while saying goodbye, she found herself repeating them. This was partly to be helpful, and partly because she felt guilty that she had been too disinterested in Jasmine's affairs to contribute anything meaningful. Sadie listened, nodding her sprouting blonde bunches and wrinkling her snub of a nose.

'Yeah,' she said. 'Your mother-in-law's right, I suppose. After all, it's her life and she's got to live it. She'll soon learn that all that glitters isn't gold.'

'True.'

'Not all beer and skittles.'

'As you and I well know – don't we, sweetie?'

'Yeah. Mind you, I wish we didn't!'

And with that they gave each other a dig in the ribs and fell about giggling.

Chapter 11

The next day summer was back. Blue sky, sunshine and the couple next door baiting each other as they prowled their garden in vests and denim cut-offs. This time the issue was not the physical attributes of any third person. It was blasphemous irreverence perpetrated against the Great God of Creative Endeavour. From the content of their razor-sharp exchange it appeared that the previous evening she had fallen asleep ('open-mouthed and dribbling') while he was reading the latest episode of his *magnum opus*. Kate, who was wandering her own green patch drinking coffee and persecuting the snails, pricked up her ears. Then she settled herself on the grass to listen.

'Oh, for God's sake! If I dropped off I didn't realize it, OK?'

'Didn't realize you'd gone to sleep?' (Derisive laughter like a blast of radio static.) 'So now you're narcoleptic, are you? Why don't you just admit you were bored? At least that would be honest.'

'All right.'

'All right what?'

'All right, I was bored.'

There was a brief silence while the world took a deep breath. Leaves stirred, flowers trembled and Kate tightened her grip on the coffee cup. Maria, sprawled inelegantly beside her, widened her eyes gleefully.

'Whoopsadaisy!' she exclaimed in an excited whisper.

'Someone's going to get it in the neck now.'

Together they leaned towards the dividing wall, straining their ears in tense expectation. And as they did so the words came, each one a jagged shard of broken glass that mangled vocal cords and ripped at vulnerable tissue. Propelled by outrage and wounded pride they detonated like warheads splattering the warm air with blood-streaked spittle.

'You bitch! You fucking bitch!'

Yet no sooner was he launched than she shot him down.

'Oh, for God's *sake*!' was the contemptuous retort. 'Give us a break, will you?'

At this point the dynamics of their marital tension changed. There was an audible whoosh as he sucked back anger and resentment and deposited them in a bunker of icy reserve.

It was silent aggression time now.
The end of the entertainment.

Which made it all a bit of a damp squib, really.

Maria, who had been trailing Kate all morning, was particularly disappointed. The vicarious delight she took in the discord of others was one of her less attractive traits, and Kate told her so. Annoyed by this rebuke, she stomped off leaving Kate stretched out on the sofa alone. But Kate did not miss her. For no sooner had Maria's rotund form vanished than she was back in Rome, returning again to a visit she paid to the Forum a week or so before leaving.

It was a day of dizzying heat (in fact, it was the way the sky viewed through dusty glass gave the impression of a heat-haze that triggered the reverie). Light-headed, consumed with the anxiety of her impending departure, she had wandered like a disembodied emanation of herself, numb to the lonely and romantic majesty of the ancient stones. Apart from an encounter with a stray dog (it growled and bared its fangs at her), it was the three stalwart matrons foraging for wild garlic and herbs among dark acanthus leaves that made the occasion memorable. Turning in unison at her approach, they fixed her with a shrewd collective stare. Then one of them took a fistful of lozenge-shaped leaves from a basket and thrust them into her hand.

'You are suffering, I can tell,' she lisped toothlessly. 'Boil these for five minutes and drink the tisane. The taste is bitter but the effect is sweet. You shall see.'

Kate was surprised and grateful. She gazed at the heavy, black-clad bodies and saw a buttressed barricade challenging all fear and uncertainty. At which point she had to restrain herself from leaping into their midst and sandwiching herself among them.

In thrall to the seductive pull of memory Kate fumbled for a cushion and hugged it to her chest. But the knowledge that she spent too much time holed up in the flat forced her to toss it aside again and open her eyes.

'Enough of this nonsense,' she told herself firmly. 'I'm going out.'

And she did. First to the corner shop for a paper, and then for a stroll along the Holloway Road. She ended up in the churchyard opposite the library, sharing a sunny bench with a vagrant who was huddled into a heavy winter coat. He had a tangled mane of shoulder-length grey hair, a vigorous grey beard and he was reading a paperback copy of *Moby Dick*. Kate positioned herself at a discreet distance, then opened her newspaper and began flicking through. She skipped the politics, war reports, royal updates and so on, pausing only when she came to a small item about a couple attacked by a white-tailed eagle with a six-foot wing span, while holidaying on the Isle of Skye. This bizarre and terrifying incident occurred while they were enjoying a moment of romantic intimacy in the heather: danger lurked in the most unlikely places, it seemed.

Closing the paper again she tried to imagine herself targeted by a kamikaze bird of prey. She did not get far, though, as the sight of a bride in a cream satin dress having a quick smoke with two bridesmaids at the back of the church, distracted her. As she watched them talking, smiling and flicking ash, her thoughts, fitful and erratic as always, went on a drift.

To another bride.
Another time.
Another place.

'Signora Benedetta got married in a blue cotton dress that her cousin the seamstress made,' she said dreamily, only realizing she had spoken aloud when her bench companion lowered his book and turned to look at her. Although the unexpected sound of her voice was somewhat unnerving (was this madness, she wondered?) she quickly regained composure and continued.

'Well, it was just after the war, you see. She was desperately poor and needed something she could wear again. There was also the problem of the celebration meal. After the Germans left the villagers were practically starving. Fortunately she had a neighbour who'd been a professional chef in Milan. He told her to bring him whatever she could find and he would come up with something. There were twenty-five guests, all relatives, and everyone made a contribution. Between them they came up with thirty eggs, three stringy old hens, half a lamb's carcass, three cups of flour, four large round loaves, half a cup of grated Parmesan, six salted anchovies, a small quantity of butter, half a litre of olive oil, two cups of sugar, coffee beans, olives, peppers, spinach, potatoes, wild rughetta, lemons, oranges and herbs.'

Her voice became reverent as she ticked off the precious ingredients one by one. She then went on to describe the entire menu. Which was:

Antipasto
Bruschetta topped with roasted slices of sweet red pepper.
Bruschetta topped with liver and herb pâté.
Fried green olives (big fat ones) stuffed with liver pâté and served hot.
A hot salad of diced boiled hen sautéed in oil and butter, mixed with diced peppers (cooked separately) and garnished with thin slivers of lemon rind.

First Course
Broth made from the old hens, enriched with beaten egg and flavoured with a sprinkling of Parmesan, nutmeg and finely grated lemon rind.

Main Course
Water and flour pancakes served with fingernail-size meatballs (made from minced hen's innards mixed with fragrant herbs).
Boiled hen served with *salza piccante verde* (finely chopped pickled green peppers, parsley and pounded anchovies).
Lamb roasted in a wood oven with garlic and whole branches of fresh rosemary.
Potatoes roasted in the oven with garlic and rosemary.
Chopped spinach sautéed in butter.
Wild rughetta salad.

Dessert
Balls of sweet cream (egg yolks, sugar and flour) fried golden-brown and served with thick wedges of lemon.
Sponge cakes filled with lemon cream and covered with meringue.
Oranges.
Coffee.

'It was a banquet. A miracle. Like when Christ fed all those thousands with five loaves and two fish,' she concluded with awe. 'I never get tired of hearing Signora Benedetta tell about it.'

The old man had listened to the story with unwavering attention. Now he cleared his throat with a loud harrumph and, in a gravelly and sonorous baritone, recited:

> 'O sweeter than the marriage-feast
> 'Tis sweeter far to me
> To walk together to the kirk
> with a goodly company.'

Kate was charmed. 'Oh. That's really beautiful!'

At which he smiled graciously – and promptly resumed reading his book.

In any other circumstances Kate would have felt she was being dismissed. In this instance, however, she took the withdrawal as a sign of her companion's wisdom and integrity. Instinct told her he was a man of deep resources who did not waste time prolonging contact beyond its immediate relevance. He was telling her that their interaction had been so spontaneously attuned to the moment, so meaningfully contained, that adding to it would have destroyed its symmetry. And she agreed with him. Besides which, she had nothing more to say on the subject.

By now the bride had finished her cigarette and was laughing uproariously at a remark made by one of the bridesmaids. Her head was flung back, her arms lifted, and her whole body shook with the exuberance of her mirth. It was a delightful image – earthy, unrestrained and optimistic – and it accompanied Kate as she started the walk home. It reminded her that she had been similarly high-spirited and carefree at her own wedding, fizzing with euphoria at being the centre of attention, with all the best of her future still to come. And why not, after all? She was in love, almost a mother and, to top it all, she was still so wonderfully young!

Thinking about how young/pretty/energetic/hopeful/unfettered/etcetera, she had once been (and was not any more), dampened her mood. Especially as the streets seemed suddenly to be teeming with formidably attractive and confident creatures all under the age of twenty-five. In the blink of an eye, the old, sick and lame had been swept from sight and replaced by firm-fleshed, tight-muscled, smooth-skinned youth. She was particularly demoralized by the compact thighs, high swivelling buttocks and bouncing silken hair that sauntered carelessly down the road a few feet in front of her.

By the time she arrived back at the flat Kate felt well and truly hagified. The body that had been reasonably acceptable when she started out was returning as loose bags of degenerating flesh clinging desperately to a shrinking and stiff-jointed frame. Her brittle locks were coming out in handfuls and her epidermis rivalled that of the proverbial prune.

Yikes!

Slamming the door behind her she rushed straight to the bathroom. There – lights blazing, nose two inches from the glass – she subjected her face to intense and anxious scrutiny. She found thread veins, the odd mole, a sprinkling of downy hairs on her upper lip. For the rest, she was still pretty wrinkle-free. But now that the chill was on her she could not be reassured.

'It means nothing,' she groaned to Maria (who had popped up again and was peering into the mirror with her). 'The buggers are like fissures in the substrata of rock. I can feel thousands of them lurking.'

Maria was a veteran of age-related obsessions. Next to

Garzanti's *Medical Encyclopaedia* her favourite reading was *Novella Duemila*, a weekly gossip magazine devoted to the carryings-on of the rich and famous. She liked it mainly for the scandal, but also because it regularly revealed which stars were walking around with beauty and sex appeal surgically enhanced. Thanks to this publication she was now an enthusiastic expert on the ins and outs of nips, tucks and silicone implants.

'Look at it this way,' she said, pleased at the opportunity to hold forth. 'At the end of the day there's always the knife. Take Cher. I mean, that woman's a wonder of cosmetic science. She's had her—'

'Listen,' Kate interrupted, watching the sour purse of her lips as she spoke. 'I don't want to hear about Cher. She's got bloody millions. I haven't!'

Later, on a restless odyssey through the parallel world of sleep, Kate found herself standing at the foot of a bed where a couple lay embracing. The woman's long red fingernails were curved like scythes and rested on her partner's bare shoulder. As she watched, the nails detached from the fingers, turning into slugs that began a slow, wriggling descent down the length of his back.

'Hey!' she demanded, surfacing briefly. 'Is this about plastic surgery or what?'

But before Maria, Lidia, or anyone else for that matter, could enlighten her, she had rolled over and was asleep once more.

Chapter 12

September 23 was Sadie's boyfriend's twenty-fifth birthday. Although she never had a good word to say about Pete, Sadie had embarked on elaborate preparations to celebrate his first quarter century in style. There was to be a catered cordon bleu buffet (fresh poached salmon, galantine of veal, wild mushroom mousse, fruit *brûlée*, etcetera). The firm was also providing a small posse of uniformed waitresses to hand out canapés and make sure no one's glass ran dry. There would be live music in the form of an up-and-coming female jazz singer called Sam Black and Pete's own amateur rock band, Lines of Descent, would take over when she finished at twelve.

'I didn't know Pete was a musician,' Kate murmured, surreptitiously sliding her tongue around the inside of the cup to savour the last delicious drops of Luigi's bitter, black coffee.

'He's not, he just thinks he is,' Sadie replied, with her usual irritated contempt. 'But I let the poor sod keep his illusions.'

Kate received her formal invitation two weeks before the event. She gave it the briefest of glances, then hid it behind Heather's grandfather's retirement clock which stood in the centre of the living-room mantel. As she told Mad Max when she went into the garden to sniff the roses, social engagements – and most particularly parties – belonged to a distant and estranged past. The world she now inhabited was a pseudo-world, a world of illusion, a world that mimicked life amid the shadowy tombs of a monumental graveyard.

While she talked, Mad Max gazed at her through sleepy slits and flicked his tail. He knew full well that underneath the fancy words Kate's problem was another. Which was that she could not face the thought of dolling herself up to meet a whole lot of strangers. His condescending indifference enraged her. 'And even if that's true,' she snapped defensively, stomping off, 'so bloody what?'

Help came from a magazine article which urged her to forget fashion, and dress according to the woman she was feeling on any given day (certainly more inspirational than comparing herself to page after page of young and impossibly perfect models). She happened upon this piece while sitting in the kitchen dunking chocolate biscuits into her ten o'clock cup of tea. She thought about it on and off for the rest of the morning and eventually decided it was worth a try. So, after completing her various domestic chores, she stripped naked in front of the full-length mirror in the bedroom and subjected her body to a painstaking inspection.

She surveyed her arms, back, breasts, belly, legs and rump, as well as the hair nestling in her armpits and covering her pubes. She crossed and uncrossed her arms, placed a hand on one hip, placed hands on both hips, stuck out her chest, stuck out her bum, tilted her head this way and that way and so on for the best part of an hour. Eventually she had to acknowledge that she had a serious problem. Which was quite simply that she felt like no woman at all. At which point Heather appeared. 'If you don't know what sort of woman *you* feel like,' she suggested, 'why not try being me?'

Hmm!

Sons, Lovers, Etcetera

* * *

The advantage of being Heather was the choice it offered. Heather was a born chameleon, the ultimate quick-change artist, mistress of a hundred and one faces. There had been the career girl, hippie layabout (eight months in Mykonos), hard-line feminist, sex kitten, punk raver, political dyke (the vegetarian café period), keep-fit fanatic and now, of course, she was Mrs Whatsit. In fact, her ability to remake herself and her opinions was such that almost every time they met Kate had been obliged to make her acquaintance anew. Some of her incarnations were more successful than others. The year she was involved with a fringe theatre director, for example, she became pretentiously arty and a compulsive name-dropper. On the other hand, living with a gardener had stimulated a practical creativity that found expression in knitting, jam-making and baking bread.

It was Heather the Trendy Sophisticate, however – perfected during the eighteen months she had worked as Girl Friday to a fashion photographer – that Kate had admired the most. Her first introduction to this glamorous persona was via a polaroid snap showing her friend perched on a bar stool wearing a slinky dress (Jean Muir) and toying with a fancy cocktail. A few months later she was in London to enrol Lorenzo on a course to improve his English and they met for lunch at a Covert Garden wine bar. On this occasion Heather was wearing a ruched, dove-grey jumpsuit in a material that looked like parachute silk. It was incredibly stylish with pockets and zips everywhere and Kate wished more than anything that it was hers.

Unfortunately the jumpsuit was not among the clothes Heather left behind (and which Kate had folded into plastic bags and stuffed under the bed). These were an eclectic jumble of bits and bobs deemed unsuitable for her new life in New York but which she could not bring herself to throw away. Most of the things were far too big but Kate tried them on anyway. She pushed up sleeves, rolled up trouser bottoms, played with collars, added and discarded belts and twisted this way and that in an effort to see herself from every angle. In the end she selected a low-cut black top and teamed it with a stretchy skirt in a leopard-skin print. 'There!' she said, striking a triumphant pose. 'If I have to go to the party, I'll go as Heather the "I don't give a damn" tart.'

Brave words. When the actual day arrived, she lost her nerve and buried herself in the buttressed garrison she had made of her bed. It was Maria who had the job of coaxing her out and getting her dressed. It was Heather who had to supervise the shaky application of mascara, lipstick and dusky peach blusher. And it was Lidia, peering over half-moon reading glasses, who shook her head sadly and sighed, '*Povera figlia.* Nobody would believe the courage it takes for a woman to have fun sometimes.'

In the taxi Kate chain-smoked, bit her nails and worried that her lipstick was too pink. She also meditated on courage: what was it? Had she ever had it? Would she be able to find it again? The answer to the first question was easy. Courage was the opposite of everything she was feeling at that moment. The answer to the second was twice. Once when she placed herself between Lorenzo and what she thought was a stampeding bull (it turned out to be a cow trotting home), and on the occasion she tongue-lashed a burly youth who tried to mug her, reducing him to repentant tears.

To question three, however, she had to admit it was very unlikely. Over the last ten years courage had been conspicuously absent from her life. In fact, this last decade had for her been characterized by a sharp increase of moral and physical cowardice and a corresponding decline in everything else. This, of course, made sense. As Miss Soloway, her much-loved English teacher (who was also an intrepid rock climber) used to say, 'In any endeavour courage is the crucial thing. All goes if courage goes.'

Remembering this Kate squared her shoulders, stiffened her spine and bared her teeth in a valiant smile. Fortunately this grim rictus was knocked from her face when the taxi swung round a corner and jolted to a halt.

Sadie's house was an imposing early Victorian mansion situated in a leafy cul-de-sac in Ladbroke Grove. A curved drive led to broad steps at the top of which stood two stone urns filled with geraniums, and a pillared portico sheltering a brass-knockered front door. Every window blazed with light and a uniformed waitress stood ready to welcome guests with a glass of Dom Perignon as they entered the spacious hall.

Kate arrived at nine on the dot and the place was already choc-a-bloc with people having a shrieking good time. Clutching her champagne like a talisman she set off in search of her hostess. She looked first into a comfortable TV room/study (where a girl in a short blue dress perused titles on a bookshelf while her companion stood beside her stroking her behind), then followed the festive clamour to a huge living room. Tall French windows were open on a small garden, which, for the occasion, had been taken over by a red and white striped marquee housing the refreshments. And it was there – flushed, perspiring and swaddled in black silk – she found her.

'Good on you, you made it!' shrieked Sadie, who had half expected Kate to chicken out. 'And just look at that sexy leopard-skin skirt!' Which, to Kate's embarrassment, various people did, including the classic blonde beauty with whom Sadie was deep in conversation and whom she introduced as Grace.

The subject of their discourse, resumed immediately the presentations were over, was film directors. Or more specifically, a particular film director Grace had recently fucked and never wanted to fuck again. In fact, so strong were her feelings on the matter that she felt driven to make sure every other female she encountered was warned. 'Whatever you do,' she said, laying a manicured hand on Kate's arm and stressing each word for emphasis. 'Don't go to bed with Howard Jacks. I did and, believe me, it's nothing less than a miracle that I'm here to tell the tale.'

Kate's first reaction was to be flattered that she should be considered eligible for such an exalted tryst. The second was curiosity. Was he a psychopath? Was his bed a casting couch for snuff movies? 'Nothing so banal,' replied Grace, lowering her voice darkly. 'It's his foreskin. The man has literally yards of the stuff. During fellatio – on which, I have to tell you, he insists – it slithers down the throat like a discarded silk stocking. I wouldn't be surprised if choking on that epidermal landslide wasn't responsible for his first wife's death.'

Yuk!

Such was the effect of this vivid description that for a moment the three women felt Howard Jack's phantom penis ballooning in their mouths. The sensation was indescribably horrible and while it lasted they could not speak. Sadie was the first to recover.

'My personal opinion of oral sex' she said, her throat sounding a little constricted, 'is that it's much nicer being done to than doing.'

Grace sighed and shook her head. 'If only it was that

simple. The truth is it all depends on who's doing the doing. If you know what I mean.'

Kate did. It was a long time since she had given a thought to fellatio or cunnilingus, yet it struck her that Grace's statement could be applied to most of life's important issues.

Talking about Howard Jacks's monstrous member had the further effect of stimulating their hunger. By now a crowd had gathered round the long refectory table, so it took time and a certain amount of jostling before they were able to pile their plates. They had just emerged victorious – Kate's mouth crammed with cream cheese and caviar tartlets – when Pete himself sauntered over. He was, indeed, tall and skinny but he had a pleasant, good-natured face and Kate thought that Sadie's description of him as a stick insect with acne a little unfair.

'Hi there, birthday boy,' Grace said, giving him a kiss and an elegantly wrapped present the size of a matchbox. 'Open it later when you're alone, OK?' Her wink and his knowing chuckle informed anyone interested that the diminutive package contained an illegal substance. Kate herself had decided against bringing a gift, considering it inappropriate as she did not know him. Now, however, she felt conspicuously empty-handed. To make things worse, she mumbled 'Happy Birthday' with a mouth still full of tartlet, and sprayed a shower of pastry crumbs over his chest.

'Thanks,' he said graciously for both the gift and Kate's felicitations, and went on to introduce the young man who was with him. 'This here is my new mate, Sean. We spent a whole fucking hour in a same dole queue yesterday. First I smoked his fags, then I nipped out and got a packet and he smoked mine.'

'Sounds like a nice little social club you've got there,' Sadie said, ominously bright.

'All depends how you approach it,' Pete replied smoothly. 'Attitude is all, sugar plum. Didn't you know?'

Sean was the same age as Pete but looked no older than sixteen. Around five-seven, he had crisp, curly black hair, smooth pink cheeks and inky-blue eyes so thickly fringed they looked like pools in a tropical rain forest. Like Kate he knew no one at the party, so when Grace moved off to mingle and Sadie took Pete aside for a private word, they stayed together. As a conversation-opener Kate asked what sort of job he was looking for.

'Whatever I can get,' he replied morosely. 'The trouble is my only work experience is helping my mother run her mobile refreshment van – I do the teas, coffees and soft drinks while she gets on with the sausage sandwiches and that sort of thing. But two months ago she took up with this bloke and told me I had to clear out. Until then there's only ever been the two of us. She'd always said all males except me were chauvinistic sputum and her only reason for seducing my father was to get his sperm.' At this point Sean became emotional. He produced a crumpled Kleenex and loudly blew his nose. 'Now the fucker uses my bedroom for his CB radio rig and I share a squat with seven others. Can you believe that?'

Kate, whose own heart had been torn from the root by Lorenzo's departure, listened in shocked belief. That a mother could so cruelly throw her son to the wolves was totally alien to her sensibilities. 'It's hard for me to understand,' she said at last. 'I too have a son, and when he decided to leave home I was . . . I am . . . oh, God!'

Now it was Kate's turn to get emotional. Her eyes filled with tears and the pulse in her throat fluttered like a trapped bird. It was an important moment for it communicated everything about each other they usefully needed to know.

Sean was the orphaned child. Kate the mother bereft.

They were a perfect fit.

Chapter 13

The next morning Kate awoke thinking of Lando. She was not pleased, and lay staring at the ceiling helpless with irritation.

But memories are like burrs.
Like it or not, they stick to you.

Two years after forsaking marital fidelity for her summer romance with Pietro, Kate took Lando as her occasional lover. The liaison continued until almost the day she left Rome for England. They first met when she was twenty-six and he eighteen, at the house of a Cuban woman who claimed to have been Che Guevara's last mistress. It was an evening of oppressive heat. For three days the sirocco had been blowing in from the Sahara, powdering the city with brick-red sand as fine as dust. Even Kate's white dress (cinched at the waist with the blue and silver belt Daniele had brought her back from Guatemala) was speckled with it. For Lando – who thought she looked like a Tartar princess – it was love at first sight. Kate, however, despite sitting next to him at dinner, hardly noticed him.

Lando spent the next six years trying to remedy this. He tried dazzling her with his radical politics (hinting at connections with the Red Brigade), amusing her with outrageous wit (reciting the jingles he composed as an advertising copywriter), inspiring her with musical talent (singing Beatles songs), affecting her with his sensitivity and perception (denouncing Daniele for not valuing the uniquely wonderful woman he'd got).

That she was married with a child did not deter him in the slightest. Quite the contrary, in fact. He had grown up in a family dominated by large, fleshy matriarchs whose deep bosoms and mossy armpits trailed intoxicating odours of talcum powder and fecund sweat. He loved the yeasty warmth of their enveloping presence and his adolescent imagination had been fertilized by the intimation of dark, moist mysteries beneath their respectable skirts. As a result, young girls did not interest him and never would. It was women, with their complications and entanglements, that inflamed his hungry libido.

Kate, although flattered by such a determined suit, was not interested. At first it was because she still believed in marital fidelity. Later there were a host of other reasons. Principal among these was the skin-crawling tone of sibilant crooning he adopted when talking to her. There was also the fact that, despite a classic profile and abundant copper-coloured hair, she was put off by the shortness of his legs.

Maria (who had short legs herself) thought Kate was being uncharitable, nit-picking and petty. 'Anyway, take my word for it,' she said crossly. 'Tenacity always wins out.'

And she was right, of course.

It happened one Sunday afternoon when Daniele was away on an assignment and Lidia had taken Lorenzo to the park. Lando wandered into the Piazza del Pantheon (he lived a couple of streets away) to find Kate sitting on the steps of the fountain eating an ice-cream and looking lonely and depressed. It was the chance meeting he had been waiting for and instinct told him this time he was going to make it. Sitting beside her, he launched into the story of a fat priest killed in that very piazza when a bolt of lightning struck the silver cross he wore around his neck. He followed this tale with the account of a nun whose eyes were plucked out by a kamikaze pigeon while she sheltered from a thunderstorm under the Pantheon's portico. Kate didn't believe any of it.

'It's true,' Lando protested. 'God looked down his celestial telescope and saw they were the devil's agents in disguise. So he punished them. I know because Old Marietta told me.'

Old Marietta was a local character. Aged between seventy and eighty, she wore long, dirty, flowered skirts over a broken pair of men's lace-ups and hawked fading roses and holy pictures around bars and restaurants. 'You mean she actually talked to you?' Kate was surprised. 'I thought she only told people to bugger off.'

'It's different with me, I've known her all my life. Before she became crazy she was the wife of a rich haberdasher and my grandmother did her laundry.'

'Really?' This time Kate really was impressed.

'Cross my heart,' Lando replied.

Then he smiled. It was a combination of his eagerness, her despondence and the fact that she had nothing better to do that clinched it. A few minutes later they were strolling back to his flat to listen to his new Milva tape. Which, of course, she never got to hear – or, at least, not on that occasion. For she had hardly got through the door when Lando came at her like a fireball propelled by a 100-m.p.h. draught. It was nothing short of an erotic hurricane.

That was how it started.
That was the way it went on.

Vida Adamoli

* * *

The ground rules were that Lando never phoned, he waited for Kate to contact him. Which, for a while, she did about once a week. But then it became once a month, and with the passing of time even six months could pass without her arranging a meeting. Although Lando accepted this state of affairs, lack of regular contact meant their relationship never got a chance to flesh out and develop. Kate continued to see him for the simple reason that he was always there. And Lando was there because the long years of waiting had prepared him for infrequency. Most crucially, however, he stayed the course because the romance existed first and foremost in his imagination.

At each encounter Kate was recreated as his unattainable object of desire. He did this by an obsessive evocation of the key erotic moments that had punctuated his six years of marking time. Although Kate knew these honed and polished memories were the emotional and sexual devices Lando needed to get off, she found listening to them progressively distasteful. This was because the fragments of her history commandeered and reworked for his fantasy soon belonged to him more than they did to her. At each tryst he managed to take away the authenticity of her life and rewrite her as a fictional character in his.

As she said to Maria, 'The price I pay for a screw with Lando is not being real.'

The reason Kate woke up thinking of Lando was because of a dream. She was back in his whitewashed bedroom looking out of the window at sunlit terracotta rooftops and a shimmering Roman sky. Then she noticed a terrace with a red and white striped awning obliquely opposite.

Sons, Lovers, Etcetera

A man and a woman were sitting at a small table eating croissants with dollops of apricot jam and whipped cream. At first she thought it was Signor Andino, Lorenzo's old Maths teacher, and his Romanian wife. When she looked more attentively, however, she realized it was none other than her cheating husband and Louisa. At that moment Lando appeared at her side and enveloped her in a blind flurry of tumultuous caresses. What's sauce for the goose is sauce for the gander, Kate thought vengefully. Now I'll give him a taste of his own medicine! Unfortunately, however, she did not get to see Daniele put in his cuckold's place. Almost immediately she was jolted awake by her erstwhile lover metamorphosising mid-embrace into Sean.

And this she found distinctly disturbing.

As it so happened, Sean was at that moment snoring happily on the living-room sofa. They had left the party shortly before midnight and he insisted on accompanying her home. She invited him in for sweet milky coffee and at 2 a.m. he was still there, eating biscuits and unburdening his soul. By which time Kate suggested it was rather late to start tramping the three or so miles to his Kentish Town squat, and asked if he wanted to stay.

He did.

So out came sheets and blankets and together they made up a bed on the sofa. Then while Kate was out of the room Sean quickly stripped off his (very unsavoury) Y-fronts and hopped in. She returned to find him with the covers decorously pulled up to his chin.

'Comfortable?'

'Mmm!'

'Well, goodnight then. Sleep well.'

'You bet.'

He looked so appealingly young and tousled, so pleased

with the way things had turned out, it was all Kate could do not to plant a smacking kiss on his forehead before tucking him in. She took a last lingering look, then closed the door softly behind her.

Sean slept like a baby and did not stir until half past twelve. By that time Kate had already handwashed the socks and underpants (it took three changes of hot soapy water and five rinses before she was satisfied they were clean). She had also been to the corner shop to buy eggs, bacon, sausages, orange juice, yoghurt and a large loaf of thick-cut sliced white bread. Her intention was to feed him a proper English fried breakfast. But Sean, it turned out, was not partial to the way the white went rubbery on fried eggs, so she cooked him a bacon omelette with grilled sausages instead.

Kate, not hungry herself, sat opposite him across the kitchen table and watched him eat. His appetite, she noted with approval, was excellent. As well as the orange juice and yoghurt, the omelette and sausages, he devoured five slices of toast and honey and drank a whole pot of tea. His table manners, however, left much to be desired. Head hovering inches above his plate he shovelled away with the single-minded, slurping gusto of a greedy three-year-old. And when he had finally finished, his chin was smeared with grease and he had toast crumbs and bits of omelette all down his front. Still, it was not his fault. Kate blamed his unnatural mother for that.

Brunch over, Kate washed the dishes and Sean dried – a job he did with obvious pleasure and meticulous care. Then he folded away the bedding while she went into the garden to check on his underwear which was pegged out on the line. (They were still a little damp so she finished them off in the oven.) Afterwards they played cards – knock-down whist and gin rummy – until Sean switched on the TV at seven and Kate grilled the rest of the sausages and bacon to serve with the baked beans she made for their supper. *Easy Rider*, which they both wanted to watch, came on at 11.30 and finished at 1.45 a.m. By which time, Kate had decided, it was too late for Sean to return to the dank doss-house he was forced to call home. So out came the sheets and blankets and once again Kate hovered vigilantly until Sean was safely bedded down.

Although usually out for the count well before midnight, Kate was not tired. It was contentment, though, rather than Heather's lumpy bed or any underlying anxiety, that kept her awake. Her mind did a video replay of the events of the day; pausing, rewinding, fast-forwarding as she savoured its details all over again. She lingered particularly over the moment while watching TV that Sean had reached across to hold her hand. It was a sweet and trusting touch that bridged a chasm and restored order and rightness to her world.

That reconnected her. Plugged her back in.

Through the half-open window a light breeze carried the sounds of young voices in conversation across the street; traffic on the Holloway Road, the floorboards creaking above her head as the bachelor upstairs paced to and fro. She listened to them without irritation. Quite the contrary, they charmed her as much as wind rustling leaves, waves pounding a beach, the straining timber of a pitching galleon.

'A pitching galleon?!' exclaimed Maria.

'All right, I know,' Kate muttered defensively. 'But I'm happy, OK?'

'*Gesù mio. Aiutaci tu!*'

Chapter 14

Sean was not fat but he was not exactly slim, either. His bones were wrapped in a soft, insulating layer of pale adipose that billowed gently around his middle and hung like a pouting lower lip over the heavy, brass-buckled belt he wore with all his trousers. Except for his shoulders and a prominent collar-bone, his was a body of no sharp corners. Flesh encircled his chest, rippled lightly across the elastic arches of his splayed ribs and flowed seamlessly from his soft belly into the cushioned buttresses that gave the back view of his buttocks the shape of a lumpy V. In jeans, T-shirt and studded black leather jacket, he appeared merely a little overweight. Naked, however, the excess of blubbery tissue blurred the edges of his masculinity and gave his body an androgynous and rather vulnerable air.

Kate found this very appealing. It spoke directly to the maternal animal tethered somewhere deep in her vortex by heartstrings of sinewy steel. This fire-breathing, crested dragon was hard to live with – especially when every now and then its tail-lashing restlessness provoked mournful howls that burst forth from her throat in an unstoppable volley. This had happened only two weeks earlier while preparing for bed after the ten o'clock news. It was that terrible need again, the longing that could not be quenched. (And all brought on by a postcard from Lago di Tevignano saying, 'Here for a couple of days to get away from Dad. Wish you'd come and sort things out.

Carina says hello. Lots of love . . .')

Lidia, who kept an eye on Kate at such moments, listened to the piteous wailing and shook her head. 'What a ferocious appetite that beast of yours has,' she commented, 'it's starvation, *mia cara*, that's driving it to such despair.'

Which was all very well, but how was she supposed to feed it?

The first time Kate bathed Sean was exactly eight days after Pete's twenty-fifth birthday bash and the day he collected sleeping bag, guitar, SF comics, etcetera, from his squat and officially moved in. It happened quite naturally. She had just finished washing his clothes – found festering malodorously in a black plastic bin liner – when he called to her from the bathroom. She arrived to find him hunched over in the tub trying to get the flannel between his shoulder-blades. 'I must have short arms,' he said, with one of his most sheepish and appealing grins. 'Give us a hand, will you?'

Kate (who had supervised all of Lorenzo's bath-times until, at the age of sixteen, he eventually got rid of her by ignoring her knocks on the locked door), was more than happy to comply. In the short time they'd known each other a comfortable intimacy had been established. So much so that it seemed right and proper she should help in this way. Furthermore, it also seemed right and proper that she should do it her way. 'I think,' she said briskly, rolling up her sleeves, 'I'll start by washing that greasy hair.'

Kate was good at washing hair, whipping up drifts of shampoo foam that peaked and swirled around his head doing its cleansing business with aerated fervour. This process was repeated twice, followed by the application of an expensive conditioner – containing Pro-vitamin B5 which supposedly penetrated the hair shaft of dry, damaged or chemically treated hair. Not that Sean's black locks were dry, damaged or chemically treated. Quite the contrary. Each strand sprang with buoyant, silky health to curl and twine and slither between her deftly massaging fingers.

Once satisfied that the hair was squeaky clean, Kate turned her attention to the rest of him. Slowly and meticulously she began scrubbing her way from neck to chest, from chest to arms, from arms to back, from back (avoiding the genital region, of course) to legs and, finally, feet. It was a rigorous scouting of the land. By the time she had finished Sean's surface configuration and all its relevant topographical details had been carefully noted. She had traced the map of his body and, by familiarizing herself with the various moles, scars, discolourations, etc., something of him was now hers.

Sean submitted to all this attention with eyes closed and mouth slack, in a state of trancelike bliss. Indeed, he was so tranquillized that when the ablutions were over and it was time to get out, all he could manage was a weak protesting moan. Kate gazed fondly at his glistening steam-pink body, his retracted penis snuggled like a plump, rosy acorn in its bristling nest of pubic hair. 'Come on, lazybones, you don't expect me to carry you, do you?' she said, pulling the plug on him and trying to sound firm. Then she adjusted her sleeves, dried her hands and went to put on the kettle for tea.

Ah! Happiness.

Sadie would not believe Kate and Sean were not having an affair. 'It's nothing to be ashamed of,' she said when they met for one of their regular rendezvous at Luigi's. 'Almost every woman I know is having it off with a younger man – even Meredith Crosby, if you can believe it! She told me just the other day that her twenty-two-year-old lover has given her more screws over the last couple of months than Richard has in ten years. I introduced you to old tortoise-face at my party, remember? He told that story about a pigeon shitting on his top hat at Eton.'

Kate nodded, seemingly attentive. In truth, she was hardly listening. Her lack of interest in the fact that Meredith Crosby now equated orgasm with two sweaty bodies zipped into a nylon sleeping bag was partly due to having met the woman only once, and partly to a natural puritanism she tried to repress but that every so often resurfaced. Overwhelmingly, however, it was due to the endocrinological upheaval Sean's arrival had triggered.

Extraordinary and unbelievable though it might seem, Kate now inhabited the body of a woman who had recently given birth. There was the contented post-partum lassitude that accompanied her from the time she got up to the time she went to bed at night. There was the fact that her breasts had grown half a size and the pale skin was now marbled with a faint tracery of blue veins. The ultimate proof had been given to her that very morning. While attending to her toilet she glanced down to see a globule of milky fluid trembling like a dewdrop on the nipple of her left breast.

Sadie's voice droned on. Behind an encouraging smile Kate's mind cut loose, following a trail of images that took her from dripping udders to latex-oozing rubber trees to big fat scoops of ice-cream. The ice-cream caused her to change tack again and she found herself remembering something that had happened many years earlier at Rome's Luna Park funfair. It was a warm afternoon in late spring. Daniele had taken Lorenzo (wearing his sheriff's star and gun holster) to sample some of the more dizzying rides. After they'd gone off Kate bought herself a vanilla ice-cream and repaired to a bench to enjoy it. Next to her, another mother fed a similar cone to a plump, dark-haired toddler. The voracious passion with which he was slurping it soon had them both laughing. '*E proprio goloso lui!*' his mother said, as proud of his greed as she was of everything else about him.

Fifteen years on Kate contemplated the little boy's face imprinted on Luigi's dusty window. There was a quality about him that reminded her of Sean. 'Why don't I take Sean to the fair,' she found herself thinking. 'I just know he'd love it.'

Sean responded to the suggestion enthusiastically. And by happy coincidence he knew of a fête due to be held in Kennington Park that very weekend. They went on Saturday October 6, a drizzly autumnal day four days after he had moved in and two and a half months into Kate's repatriation. The wet grass was strewn with sweet wrappers, drink cans and sodden drifts of fallen leaves. The sky was a sagging canopy of blotting-paper grey. Gazing at the jumble of stalls glimpsed beyond the indoor swimming pool, Kate felt her enthusiasm falter slightly. Not so Sean.

'Vroomm vroomm *vroomm*!' he cried, skipping along with his arms held stiffly in front of him and turning an imaginary steering wheel. 'Bumper cars here I come!'

The fair had a dodgems, a Ferris wheel, an inflatable castle, a couple of roundabouts – one with rockets and lunar modules – rifle-ranges and various lucky dips. Kids shrieked, music blared and a smell of frying onions and burnt fat permeated the air. The first thing Sean wanted to do was show Kate what a crack marksman he was. (out of five shots four hit the target and he won a pink fluffy rabbit.) Next he wanted a hot dog, candyfloss and a ride on the dodgems – in that order. Kate, who found bumper cars scary, refused to have a go but promised to watch him from the sidelines. She took up position near a trio of pre-teen girls who were following the aggressive posturing of some older boys with flirtatious delight. 'Get a load of the arsehole in number 4!' one of them screeched.

'Yeah,' said her friend, giggling and dragging on a cigarette. 'He fancies himself rotten.'

Across from the bumpers, next to a stall selling incense and crystals, was the tent where Madame Semiramis told fortunes for five pounds. Madame Semiramis, wearing a fake leopard-skin jacket over a cerise dress, was sitting with splayed knees on a canvas chair by the entrance flap. She was short and plump with dark curly hair and she looked so much like Maria they could have been sisters. Feeling herself observed, Madame Semiramis glanced over and stared Kate straight in the eyes. Then she smiled encouragingly and beckoned her over. At that precise moment Sean was digging in his pocket to pay for a fourth ride. The boy is having fun, Kate reasoned to herself. Why shouldn't I?

Madame Semiramis, whose real name was Fatima, was of Turkish origin. In a previous incarnation, however, she had been Queen Semiramis of Assyria, which was why she had chosen it as her professional name. She told Kate this while lighting a battered Primus which, after much coaxing and with a strong smell of paraffin, spluttered into life. The reason for lighting the stove was not to combat the damp chill, although that was a bonus, but to make coffee. In the normal course of events clients were given a tarot reading. For Kate, however, and at no extra cost, Madame Semiramis had offered to investigate her future in coffee dregs.

'It's an ancient divination art I learnt from my maternal grandmother,' she explained, spooning finely ground grains into a pot of water and putting it on to boil. 'And I only do it for people I get a special feeling about.'

'And I give you a special feeling?'

'My dear, when I saw you standing by the bumpers I got a jolt. You're a creature lost in space and time, no question about it.'

Kate recognised the 'lost in space and time' bit as a line from *The Rocky Horror Picture Show*, a film she'd seen at least four times. She had a flash vision of the sibyl in fishnets and satin teddy dressed as Little Nell, one she might have lingered on had she not been distracted by the antics of a manic cat who was making pouncing attacks on a piece of screwed-up cellophane. When the coffee was ready Madame Semiramis shooed the animal out and took her place opposite Kate at a folding card table covered with green baize.

'Do I drink the coffee first?'

'Of course,' Madame Semiramis replied solemnly. She had opaque green eyes like olives in brine. 'You wouldn't want to waste it, would you?'

So Kate drank the coffee, gave the cup three anticlockwise swirls, tipped out the remaining liquid and handed it over. Just as she was instructed. Madame Semiramis peered at the grainy sediment clinging to the sides in swirls, drifts, streaks, clumps and delicate dispersions. Then she nodded her head in a way that indicated that the arcane hieroglyphics made everything clear to her.

'Well, my dear,' she said. 'You've been through a lot. You've suffered torments for love and even now there's one particular man you can't forget. Friends you thought you could trust have turned out to be treacherous. But every cloud has a silver lining. The message here is that money, travel and love are waiting on the horizon. All these things will come to you via a man you'll meet within the next six months. I see trouble in the guise of a glamorous divorcee who will set herself up as your rival. This man won't respond, however. He will devote himself to you and fulfil all your desires,' she gave Kate's hand a sympathetic squeeze. 'Keep your chin up – good times lie ahead. I promise.'

Madame Semiramis not only looked like Maria, she gave identical readings. Indeed, it was all so nostalgic Kate's eyes began filling with sentimental tears. Madame Semiramis, who was used to women turning weepy on her, gave her hand another squeeze and refilled their cups.

'Drink!' she ordered. 'Coffee stimulates the heart and the nervous system. It increases the activity of the skin and kidneys and even acts as a mild laxative. I didn't mention it before but it was written plain that your bowels are definitely sluggish.'

Kate smiled through a watery blur. She'd got that right, at least.

On the tube going back Sean was in a sulky mood. 'Why did you go off without telling me?' he complained. 'I looked everywhere for you but you'd disappeared.'

Kate had the fluffy rabbit tucked under one arm. Its pink synthetic hair was moulting in fluorescent abundance over her grey jacket. 'Look at this !' she exclaimed. 'If a small kid got the stuff in its mouth it could be lethal.'

Sean did not reply. With a thrusting pout of his lower lip he glared at the Dateline ad over the beaded head of the black girl opposite, snarling at the promise that ninety-six per cent of people who joined would find friendship, love or marriage. Kate knew all about sulkers. Lorenzo had been a sulky child, particularly between the ages of eleven and fourteen. In her experience you either ignored them or you tried distraction. So she told him about the two old ladies (seventy if a day) she had seen shrieking with delight as they circled the sky on the Ferris wheel. When this elicited no response, she said, 'Shall I tell you what Madame Semiramis predicted was in store for me?'

Despite the indifferent shrug Kate knew she had got him. So she continued picking hairs off her jacket until curiosity won out.

'Well?' he demanded.

'Madame Semiramis says I'm about to meet a rich man who'll fall madly in love with me and dedicate his life to satisfying my needs.'

This light-hearted snippet distracted Sean more effectively than she could have anticipated. 'And you swallowed that drivel?' he cried. 'God, I can't believe how pathetic women are sometimes. My mum dragged me to some poxy gypsy once who told me to expect good news in the post. Well, the next day I got a parcel. And what was in it? A bubble-wrapped turd, that's what!'

Sean's foot was going up and down like a yo-yo. Some deep-seated insecurity – fear of abandonment, perhaps – had clearly been stirred. Kate took his hand and stroked it reassuringly.

'There, there,' she said soothingly. 'There, there.'

Chapter 15

They got back from the fair at six-fifteen and at seven Kate served supper. Sean let her tie an apron around his neck – to stop him spilling food down his shirt – then proceeded to eat three-quarters of the 10½ x 12½ inch tray of *rigatoni* (mixed with tomatoes, peas, mushrooms and mozzarella) that Kate had prepared ready for the oven that morning. He then scoffed the entire contents of a family size trifle from Tesco, to which he added dollops of extra-thick double cream. They shared a £4.75 bottle of Chianti – or rather Kate had a couple of glasses and Sean drank the rest. At ten-thirty he went to bed with the latest edition of *Classic Bikes*, a can of Special Brew and a Mars bar.

The next day his food intake broke all records. If she hadn't seen it with her own eyes Kate would never have believed anyone could eat so much without a fatal rupture of the gut. His consumption was as follows.

Breakfast: fry-up of four eggs, four rashers of streaky bacon; two bowls of Shreddies topped with sliced banana and extra-thick double cream; five slices of toast and honey, three mugs of sugary tea, several nectarines and an apple. Mid-morning: a large can of Coke, a large packet of tortilla chips, half a packet of chocolate biscuits, a banana and a Mars bar. Lunch: two tins of Heinz tomato soup with crackers, two sausage sandwiches, two peanut butter and jam sandwiches, one low-fat blackberry yoghurt, two cans of Special Brew and a Mars bar. Mid-afternoon: a can of

Special Brew, a packet of crisps, a meat pie from the fish and chip shop, two nectarines and a Mars bar. Supper: two heaped platefuls of spaghetti *carbonara* (Kate was now making regular forays to the Italian deli), two servings of tomato and onion salad, two-thirds of a French loaf stuffed with brie and salami, ice-cream and hot treacle sauce.

And a Mars bar.

They finished eating at eight and for the rest of the evening Sean lay glazed-eyed, slack-jawed and gasping on the collapsed springs of Heather's old sofa. He remained semi-comatose until eleven when his stomach called again. It gurgled, squeaked, grumbled and growled.
'Don't tell me you're hungry again!' Kate exclaimed, looking up from her magazine with an expression of horrified disbelief. 'I refuse to believe it!'
Sean responded with a lazy, self-indulgent simper. 'Not hungry exactly. But I wouldn't say no to a mug of your lovely hot chocolate.'
He pronounced 'hot chocolate' with a lascivious roll, as though his tongue was coated with liquid velvet. Kate felt the words slither into her auditory canal, reverberate on her tympanum, pass into the membranous Eustachian tube and from there take a silky slide down to the moist tissue at the back of her throat.

Where, like two fat fingers, they stuck.

Now Kate was the first to appreciate a healthy appetite. Indeed, despite the appalling table manners, Sean's voracity was one of the things she found most endearing. But with each day that passed, she had seen the appetite grow until gorging and guzzling were Sean's principal occupations. Severe postprandial discomfort – with an attendant souring of mood – was an inevitable consequence. At least five times a day he lay helpless as a beached whale; belching, sweating and complaining about the dead dog decomposing in his stomach. Even Maria, usually an advocate of no-holds-barred gluttony, was disapproving.

'That's some cuckoo you've taken into the nest and no mistake,' she said, peering distastefully at his inert bulk snoring open-mouthed on the sofa. 'The creature must have put on at least two stone since you've had him. Take my advice, *cara*. Get rid of him before he puts on another twenty and has to be winched out by crane.'

Kate immediately found herself reacting defensively (maternal hackles on the rise again). 'You don't understand,' she said. 'His mother's abandoned him. Sean's got emotional problems.'

This cut no ice with Maria. She tossed her head with a contemptuous snort.

'If that one's got anything,' she retorted. 'It's a bad case of worms.'

Lidia agreed with her. Furthermore, as a woman who knew the importance of husbanding resources, she felt it her duty to remind Kate of the financial consequences of her hospitality.

'That young man is a rat gnawing his way through your wallet,' she warned sternly. 'You're spending as much on food as a woman with a family of ten. Remember how hard it was to get Daniele to give you what you needed to come here? I know my son. Platonic or otherwise, if he should discover there's another man sharing your roof he won't part with another penny.'

This was true and Kate knew it. The money he spent on his extramarital diversions did not come into the equation.

'Double standards, just like his father,' said Lidia. 'But

that's the situation and you've got to remember it.'

Kate had arrived in London with £1,300 in cash. One thousand had been prised from Daniele's reluctant pocket, the rest was money saved from the housekeeping. Due to her pre-Sean frugality (there was one week when she managed to spend only £5.70, for example), three months later she still had £583 of it left. She kept the money inside a yellow and red striped sock – colours of La Roma football team, which Lorenzo supported. This in turn was stuffed down a single welly abandoned by Heather, at the bottom of the wardrobe.

It had become a ritual to count the wad every Friday evening before going to bed. She smoothed out the five-, ten-, and twenty-pound notes, spread them around her on the bed, counted them, collected them up and rolled them into a bundle which she then secured with an elastic band. Although it was irrational, Kate was convinced she knew which of the notes came from Daniele and which from her biscuit tin. This was because, when rubbed between thumb and forefinger, the biscuit-tin notes smelt of nothing in particular, while Daniel's were indelibly impregnated with his smell. An unmistakable odour of sweat and Nazionale cigarettes that rose from the paper like steam.

The night Sean asked Kate for hot chocolate she had a dream. She was wallowing naked with an old woman in a protected pool on a small rocky beach. Behind them was a deep, thickly wooded gorge that fell in a plunging cleft down to the cove. It was late afternoon. The sun was lost behind great turreted edifices of brooding cloud. The sea was rough, crashing against steep walls of rock and throwing up exploding waterfalls of frothy spume. The water, dark blue streaked with aquamarine and turquoise, seethed and sucked and heaved through the outcrop of boulders to where they lay. It was like being in a jacuzzi.

The old woman was in her eighties. Her head was large and square with a thatch of stiff grey hair held off her face with a black velvet headband. Her shoulders were narrow – barely wider than her face – but the flesh of her upper arms billowed out, giving the impression of a second set of shoulders a little lower down. The huge breasts (slung into a blue and white patterned bikini) and enormous belly together formed an almost perfect sphere and were covered by skin as brown and shiny as a chestnut. Her legs, however, short and stubby though they were, were straight and strong with firm, rounded thighs and not a trace of a varicose vein. It looked as though a pair of young limbs had been grafted on to an aged body.

The old woman was Signora Pina, Lidia's lifelong friend and café companion – although never having seen her semi-naked before it was a moment before Kate recognized her. When she did, however, she could not have been more pleased. This was partly because she was fond of Signora Pina, but also because her presence gave Kate a clue to the significance of the dream.

'I understand!' she cried, clapping her hands with delight. 'This is all about financial restraint and the wisdom that comes with Glorious Widowhood!'

But Signora Pina shook her large, grey head. 'No, dear,' she replied serenely. 'This is all about breaking wind.'

And with that the old woman expelled a great storm of bubbles that rose to the surface of the water and began gaily pinging and popping all around her.

Kate awoke enveloped in a warm cloud of intestinal gas. She also woke up a different woman from the one she had been the night before. For at some point between midnight and 8 a.m. a plug had been pulled and something had drained away. She sensed this the moment the grey morning light filtering through the cotton curtains hit her retina. The feeling grew as she got out of bed, pulling a cardigan over the track suit that, with the arrival of autumn, she'd started wearing as pyjamas. And it hit her full force when she entered the kitchen where Sean, in a haze of burnt fat, was shovelling breakfast down his throat.

Whatever it was that had left her during the night, its absence made Kate feel lighter and more in control. It had also peeled a layer from her eyes, obliging her to turn a focused and unblurred gaze on the world (at that moment limited to the untidy kitchen and Sean). Leaning against the sink, arms crossed and head tilted, she sipped her coffee and calmly observed. What she saw was a snorting creature gobbling at the trough, its greasy suckers working as avidly as any leech filling its crop. There was no avoiding the fact – and neither did she want to – that Sean had blossomed into a monstrous flower.

A bloated tuber.
An engorged organ for the storage of food.

Ugh!

With the disgust, however, came an unwelcome recognition. And a great wodge of guilt. For she knew that while Sean stuffed himself on the food she prepared, her longing for a substitute child fed rapaciously off his willingness to be fussed over and nurtured. She was the Monstrous Mother. This Monstrous Baby was her own creation. And if she could do this to Sean, what would she have done to Lorenzo if he hadn't had the self-preservation to fly the nest?

Sons, Lovers, Etcetera

She shivered.
The thought was too awful to consider.

Chapter 16

Change, as they say, was in the air. And Sean soon realized it. There were no more bath-time administrations: he was left to sponge his armpits and abundant belly rolls himself. His laundry wasn't getting done and, much more importantly, neither was the cooking. He was hurt, angry and confused.

'Just what's going on around here?' he demanded, having finally realized that sulking and tantrums were getting him nowhere. 'I mean what the fuck's got into you?'

Kate contemplated his crisp, curly black hair, the smooth pink cheeks and the inky-blue eyes so thickly fringed they reminded her of pools in a tropical rain forest. She was fond of him, she wished him well, but when it came down to it he was not her baby and never could be. The symbiotic bond they had shared was no longer there.

'I think,' she said, in a voice firm but not unkind. 'That it's time you considered contacting your mother again.'

So he did. Straight away, in fact.
Which, it has to be said, took Kate rather by surprise.

And half an hour later she was there, parking her mobile refreshments van outside the flat. She brought with her an aura of fierce eccentricity and three bacon sandwiches – one each – which she produced wrapped in tin foil from the front pocket of her baggy green overalls.

'Pleased to meet you,' she said to Kate, presenting her offering. 'My name's Phil.'

Phil (short for Philippa) was a mountain to her son's molehill. She was at least six foot tall, big-hipped and broad-shouldered, with round grey eyes that looked as though they'd been tacked on to the surface of her large, flat face as an afterthought. Her hair, dyed green like her overalls, stuck up in lacquered tufts all over her head. She had coiled snakes tattooed around both wrists and a Gorgon on her left bicep.

'And it doesn't stop there,' she chuckled to Kate (when Sean was out of earshot). 'I've got Betty Boop on my clitoral hood. It takes cast-iron balls to put yourself through that, I can tell you!'

Kate, who once fainted while having a flu jab, was impressed. Indeed, she was impressed by Phil generally. It was not only her size and magnificent fearlessness, but the speed and dexterity with which she produced spindly roll-ups using one hand. They were in Heather's sitting room – Phil and Sean sharing the sofa – washing down the bacon sandwiches with half-pint mugs of strongly brewed tea. Autumnal sunshine slanting through the window illuminated dancing dust motes and gave the threadbare shabbiness a companionable and friendly glow.

'Comfortable and homely,' was how Phil described it. 'Conducive to a good chin-wag.'

She herself was in an expansive and ruminative mood. She talked about the popularity of the veggie-burger she had recently added to her menu and of discovering a shoe shop catering for transvestites (the one next to Kate's launderette) where she could get the outrageous styles she favoured in a size ten. But her main topic was Life and What a Bugger It Was. Just to put Kate in the picture she summarized her own odyssey as 'blood, sweat and fucking tears'.

Sean responded to this statement as though he was being personally attacked. He flushed, crossed his arms defensively and his lower lip trembled. Then he sniffed loudly.

'Shut up! You're such a silly arse,' growled Phil, leaning across and slamming her fist fondly into his ribs.

'Me?' Sean was indignant. 'What about that nerd you're living with then?'

'Oh, he's gone. Threw him out with the rubbish a couple of weeks ago.' At this she threw back her head and roared with laughter.

'Really?'

'That's what I said.'

'Well, if he's moved his CB rig out of my bedroom,' Sean grinned, 'then I guess I can come home.'

For the entire time during Sean's sojourn, Kate had not been visited once by her wandering pain. Neither had she been troubled by the old vortex. The connection did not escape her and waving goodbye to the lurching refreshments van she experienced a moment of dread. How long, she asked herself, before the demons struck and the whole thing started up again? She took this unpleasant thought into the garden with the intention of discussing it with Mad Max. But perverse feline that he was, Max refused to commune and kept his gaze fixed on something invisible off to his left.

Kate did not take offence. On the contrary, his regal indifference infected her with calm and well-being. Sitting back on her heels she explored these unfamiliar emotions and, possibly for the first time ever, savoured being completely alone. And while she was savouring (admiring the late-blooming roses, watching the clouds, sniffing the air, etcetera), she had a numinously inspired insight. In that moment she knew that the fearsome umbilical cord that bound her to rejection and suffering had shrivelled at the root and dropped away. Lorenzo was himself and she was herself. They were two separate beings. Suddenly it was all so simple. All the angst, all the desperate clinging on, was over. It was water under the bridge. History. Something she had definitely finished with now.

Really?
Dream on, honey. There's a long way to go yet!

She stayed in the garden until 4.15 when it started to rain, sharp needlepoints that attacked her skin like lilliputian arrows. Mad Max was immediately over the wall and hotfooting it back to wherever he went when he was not there. Kate stayed a few minutes longer to let the pummelling raindrops give her face a free massage. At 4.20 the phone rang (Sean wanted to know if his treasured fifties Zippo had slipped down the side of the sofa), and at 4.25 something was shoved noisily through the letter-box. Going to investigate, Kate found a leaflet announcing a meeting of environmental activists being held that evening at Peckham town hall. Scanning it casually the name of the visiting German Green Party representative, printed large and bold, leapt out at her. And who was it? None other than Deiter Schmidt, that's who!

Deiter Schmidt lived on in Kate's heart as her greatest unfulfilled passion. They had met seventeen years earlier when he came to Rome to speak at a conference of the Italian Radical Left. Daniele interviewed him, got drunk with him, and invited him back to the flat for dinner. He was twenty-six then, a firebrand Marxist with wild red hair and an outrageous manner. Minutes after being introduced he followed Kate into the kitchen (where she was making chick-pea and pasta soup), grabbed her round the waist and told her she was gorgeous. At table he held forth on the CIA, the Baader-Meinhof gang, revenge of the proletariat, etcetera, etcetera; a dazzling display of eloquence she recognized as a verbal mating dance that was being performed just for her.

Heady stuff, of which there was more.

Back in the kitchen (this time Kate was preparing coffee), he told her that he had fallen madly in love. 'The moment I saw you I knew you were the woman of my dreams,' he declared passionately. 'I can't deny my feelings. Nothing like this has ever happened to me before!'
   Nothing remotely like it had happened to Kate before, either. Never had she made such an instantly powerful impact. It was like a romantic fantasy gone wild. Deiter – adding hot, meaningful glances to his oratory – stayed until two in the morning, during which time her confused excitement escalated. By the time he left, her flush was so hectic that Daniele, thinking she was running a temperature, suggested she dose herself with aspirin before going to bed. And the following morning he was back. He arrived minutes after Daniele had left for the office to find her uncombed, without make-up and trying to convince Lorenzo that he couldn't wear his wellington boots because it wasn't raining.
   'Leave it to me,' Deiter said, taking over. At which he proceeded to tell Lorenzo about a boy who was so attached to his wellingtons he even wore them to bed. When his mother finally pulled them off she found a bumper crop of mushrooms had grown on his feet. Not wanting to waste them she made them into a soup for his lunch. It was the most delicious soup the boy had ever tasted and

he lapped up every last drop. No sooner had he finished, however, than he fell down dead.

'But why? Why did he die?'

'Because the mushrooms were poisonous, that's why. Mushrooms that grow in little boys' wellingtons are always poisonous. Didn't you know that?'

'Were they red like mine?'

'Yep.'

This gruesome story did not frighten Lorenzo in the slightest. He was impressed. So was Kate, who smiled at him radiantly. Not only was the main a dream suitor, he was a natural with kids!

With the crisis of footwear solved – and Kate made hastily presentable – Deiter insisted on driving them (in a battered Fiat 500 borrowed from one of the conference organizers) to a piazza near his hotel. Situated on top of a hill, it had two open-air cafés, a delightfully old-fashioned merry-go-round, and commanded a spectacular view over the green sweep of Villa Gloria, where, a century before, Garibaldi fought a bloody battle in his campaign to take Rome. Lorenzo immediately made friends with another English-speaking boy and went off to play. As the child's smartly uniformed nanny was keeping an eye on them, Kate and Dieter were able to concentrate on furthering their acquaintance at the nearest café.

Dieter, as was his wont, did most of the talking. Gulping beer and chain-smoking unfiltered Nazionali, he told her about his exploits as a student activist and his present position as high-profile spokesperson for the young militant left. He described the flat he shared with three others (big, untidy, a centre for political debate), the police harassment (raids, phone-tapping, intercepted mail) and their riotous parties (drink, drugs and rock'n'roll).

He also gave his opinion as to the state of her marriage.

'What you've got to face is that Daniele doesn't value

you the way you deserve. He's turned you into a domestic drudge and couldn't give a damn that you're wasting your potential. I mean, take last night. While you were running around fetching and carrying, what did he do? Nothing! I couldn't believe it when the guy spilt his coffee and sent you scurrying for a cloth to wipe it up!'

Kate, mortified to have shown herself such a spineless and biddable whimp, said lamely, 'That's partly his culture. Men expect to be waited on here.'

'Well, what about the way he ogles other women, then? When we went for that drink after the interview, he talked about nothing but tits and legs and arses.' Deiter reached for her hand. 'Look, I'm not telling you this to upset you, but you're wasted on him. Give your love to a man who can appreciate it. A man who will do everything to make you happy.'

Deiter was wearing an old brown leather jacket over a navy T-shirt. His blue eyes burned fiercely and the sun struck sparks from his unruly red hair. Kate thought he was magnificent – and her expression showed it.

'*Liebschen*,' Deiter murmured.

And leaning across the table he cupped her face in his hands and kissed her.

It was lingering. It was tender.
It was pure magic!

When they got back Lorenzo took a fistful of biscuits and settled in front of the TV. Deiter and Kate went out onto the terrace where he continued to press his suit. It was more of the same (expressed even more persuasively) and culminated with the plea that Kate exchange her domestic prison for a free and radical life with him in Berlin. A free and radical life in Berlin! The prospect electrified and thrilled. It was only the arrival of Daniele – driven home early by his thumping hangover – which stopped her from sinking to her knees in dizzy surrender.

'Listen, you shit,' Daniele roared – he hadn't heard all but he'd heard enough. 'If you want to start a revolution, don't do it here! Anyone throwing Molotovs in my house gets their fingers blown off! Do I make myself clear?'

He grabbed Deiter's arm, Deiter grabbed his, and a lot of shouting and shoving followed. Fortunately the altercation stopped short of an actual fight (Deiter might be an outspoken advocate of political violence, but he did his best to avoid it on a personal level). After that it was all over very quickly. Lorenzo came to see what all the noise was about and Daniele frogmarched his rival to the door.

'I meant everything I said, Kate,' Deiter called as it slammed in his face. 'I'll come back for you, I promise!'

But he didn't. Although every day for more than a year she expected him. And long after she ceased expecting him, he stayed in her thoughts. He was her big 'What if?', the unrealized promise she would never forget.

Chapter 17

At the sight of Deiter's name every emotion connected with him was reawakened. Kate's eyes raked back and forth over the leaflet, trying to take in the fact that at that very moment he was living and breathing just miles from where she stood. As she did so her mind flashed to the secret stash of press cuttings tucked under bras and knickers in her underwear drawer in Rome (most of them collected in the years immediately following their meeting, after which his prominence rapidly declined). Mentally sifting through them again, she found herself recalling her various justifications as to why he had never written or made a phone call. He'd had a crisis of conscience about wrecking her marriage, for instance; he had sacrificed personal happiness for his political mission, even that he'd got involved with a Marxist groupie who threatened suicide if he left her. But none of that counted now. All she knew was that she had to see him. Peckham was in darkest south London, and Kate had hitherto felt unable to venture further than the immediate vicinity of Heather's flat. Come hell or high water, however, and whatever the perils, this was a journey she was determined to make.

Her expedition started with a tube ride to the Elephant and Castle ('Heffalump 'n' Carsew', as a charlady briefly employed by her mother used to call it.) She shared a carriage with a party of Scandinavian tourists to Oxford

Circus, then changed to a Bakerloo line train where stony-faced passengers endured the rowdy behaviour of a posturing trio of teenage boys. At the Elephant she quickly located her bus stop, after which she waited a quarter of an hour for a number 12. When it eventually came it was half empty. Mounting the stairs behind a girl in a crotch-grazing mini she found the front-left-hand window-seat (her favourite) still unclaimed. This, she decided, was an auspicious sign.

Destiny was letting her know it was on her side.

The bus lurched off and she hugged herself tight. She was fizzing with excitement. The depth-charges planted all those years ago were reactivated and pinging off in her blood. It was like being on drugs. Everything was heightened and significant. Eyes wide and eager, she devoured the sights presented to her through the rain-spattered glass. Night – and her inflamed senses – bestowed on the Walworth and Peckham Roads a mean and scurvy glamour. Orange street lights, multicoloured shop signs and gaudy neon smeared the wet pavements with stained-glass reflections. Tail-lights from the vehicles leaked trails of blood on to the potholed, tar-black asphalt. Sound bites of music blasted forth from the open windows of passing cars.

'Everything I've ever felt or done has led me here,' she whispered to herself. 'To this seat on this bus going to Peckham, looking out at the rain. One infinitesimal instant in the eternity of time and I'm experiencing it with my fullest consciousness!'

But the second she formulated this thought, of course, it was no longer true. The present, slippery as an eel, slithered from her grasp. And before she knew it she was twenty-three again, humming a nostalgic medley of radical tunes in harmony with the chorus of voices echoing back down the years. And with each note she sang ('Give Peace a Chance', the *Internationale*, '*Bella Ciao*', etcetera), the adrenalin flowed faster. Her heart thumped, her palms sweated and her production of glucose and lipids rose.

She arrived at the town hall ten minutes after the debate had started. The large room was packed to capacity and she had to squat with other latecomers on the floor. Up on stage two women and three men were seated at a long table facing the audience. None of them looked remotely like the Deiter she had known (or conserved in her press cuttings), so she set about identifying him by logical elimination. One, he was not a woman. Two, it was unlikely that he had grown from five-foot nineish to what, seated, looked like a hulking six-four. Three he was too young to be the Bertrand Russell look-alike in the I Ran the World T-shirt. Which left only the man with hunched shoulders, thinning gingery hair and the bored, disgruntled face.

Except to note the polemical and acrimonious tone, and the fact that Deiter was disliked both by his fellow panellists and a heckling section of the audience (charisma and oratory lost with youth, it seemed), Kate paid no attention to the discussion at all. Wedging herself between someone's rucksack and the wall, her eyes telescoped in on him and there they stayed. Beginning at the top of his head and working slowly down to the booted feet sticking out from under the table, she set about deconstructing him inch by meticulous inch. And when she finished she started the whole business all over again. She was desperate to find anything, however soiled or tattered, by which she could effect a resurrection. Like a rag-picker crawling over a refuse mountain, she foraged for a gesture/expression/flash of spirit that she could pull from the smoking rubble and turn to profit. But there was nothing. The man she had expected to meet was not there. In his place she found a rather unattractive stranger.

Poignant and anticlimactic though this was, Kate had no intention of leaving it there. After nursing her fantasy for so many years there was no way she could just walk away and forget it. Whoever or whatever Deiter was now, she still had to make contact. In the tearful aftermath of Deiter's enforced departure from their flat, Daniele had dismissed her earth-shaking, two-day romance as 'the overheating of a silly housewife by an arrogant and unprincipled shit'. Now was Deiter's chance to prove him wrong. She wanted him to light up at her approach, vaulting the decades with his welcome of joy, disbelief and celebration. But there was something else, too. If Deiter had changed beyond all recognition, what about her? She needed his warm and speedy response to reassure her that something of the girl she'd once been still survived.

None of which (surprise, surprise) happened.

She was on her feet and ready when he came off stage. Touching him lightly on the arm, she told him her name and the time and place of their acquaintance. Then, holding her breath, she waited. Deiter peered, furrowed his brow, chewed his pale lips, muttered that she was talking about 'a bloody long time ago', and eventually admitted he had no recollection of ever having seen her before.

'It's like this,' he explained with an apologetic shrug. 'I travel so much and meet so many people, I've stopped trying to keep track of anyone. Take this year, for example. Since January I've attended conferences in France, Italy,

Portugal and Sweden, as well as two in Japan. And now I'm here. I tell you – Kate, did you say your name was? – well, Kate, believe me, it's all bloody go.'

Anger, hurt, disappointment, the *monumental unfairness* of it all, hit Kate full force. Here was the man who had engaged her romantic imagination like no other, who'd been billeted in her heart for seventeen years like the *Herr Kommandant* of an occupying army – actually saying he hadn't a clue who she was! Daniele was right. His declarations, the wondrous kiss, their brief but tumultuous time together, meant nothing. As far as Deiter was concerned the whole episode had been simply a bit of erotic fun. An amusing way to pass the time. A titillating alternative to the Vatican museum. And while she was yearning and dreaming, it had been out of sight, out of mind for him.

'On my last trip to Tokyo,' Deiter continued, still justifying his amnesia, 'this guy came up to me and it was only halfway through our conversation that I realized I'd been to his place for . . .'

But although Kate appeared attentive she had ceased to hear a word he said. His voice was drowned out by the rise of her vengeful rage. Thundering like a tidal wave, it swept from the soles of her feet to the tingling roots of each erect and quivering hair. Her jaw clenched, her spine stiffened and her muscles tensed and flexed. Slowly she pulled on a black balaclava, slung a Kalashnikov over her shoulder, and stuffed a hefty .44 Magnum into her viciously spiked belt. Now was the time for action.

No more emotional bullshit.
No more pissing around.

Ever!

* * *

'Don't worry about it,' she said, interrupting his flow with a cunning and subversive smile. 'The same thing happens to me all the time. Look, I've got an idea. Why don't we renew our acquaintance over a drink?'

Deiter's face brightened. It was clear the suggestion appealed.

'Sounds good,' he grinned. 'Give me five minutes with that tall guy over there and I'll be right with you.'

By now people had started to leave. Keyed up and restless, Kate went on the prowl. Among those still hanging around debating among themselves were two women. From the sharp glances darted in Deiter's direction she knew they were talking about him. Studiedly casual, she drew close enough to listen.

'I can understand the first time – but twice!'

'I know. Especially if you think what she went through while expecting Rosie. He moved that girl into their house and told her she could like it or lump it. What a prize prick!'

'I tell you, if I were her I'd have an abortion. After all, it's only two months.'

'Did she tell you about that geologist chap she's met? He gave her the money for the airfare back. She says they're thinking of emigrating to New Zealand.'

'More reason for a termination. Start with a clean slate, I say,'

'A clean slate? Can there ever be a clean slate after what she's been through?'

'You're right. I'll tell you something, though. One of these days a female with hobnails will come along and kick the bugger into shape.'

At that moment Deiter finished his conversation with the tall man. He waved at Kate and beckoned her over. She followed him out of the hall and into the street. From his cocky swagger it was clear he was unaware of the gun pressing into his back. Kate smiled grimly.

Povero cretino!'

Chapter 18

For Deiter it was a gift-wrapped fuck. For Kate; riding his insignificant tumescence (hair dishevelled and breasts bouncing); it was a sweaty exercise of the most urgent import. For her undercover mission was to recoup and transform the long-cherished fantasy that she existed eternally as Deiter's female ideal – the Beatrice to his Dante, the Héloise to his Abélard, the Cleopatra to his Antony. She was well aware that many would say her tenacious attachment to this romantic illusion showed emotional immaturity, and was her problem, not his. He'd behaved like a prick – so what? She lived in the real world, for God's sake. Didn't she know people behaved like pricks every day?

But Kate was not in the mood for being rational. Her ego was wounded, her fairy-story destroyed. He'd made her feel the silliest of fools. In other words, she wanted her own back. So with vaginal contractions, pelvic gyrations and a dancing tongue, she set about demolishing the soured dream and seizing control of the newly appraised reality. (And along the way she discovered that vengeance was a pretty powerful aphrodisiac when given its head.)

Deiter was going for orgasm.
Kate was going for victory of self.

* * *

Vida Adamoli

Foreplay commenced at the bar of a crowded pub round the corner from Peckham town hall. Kate bought the first round, Deiter the second, by which time, intoxicated by the scent of cunt on offer, he had become feverishly animated and twice splashed lager down the front of her dress. (It was black jersey, one of Heather's, and had been flung on after a prolonged frenzy of indecision over what to wear. Her hair, another source of agony, had been moussed, rolled, side-parted, teased into fluffy girlishness and eventually raked into a desperate topknot. Surveying her reflection in the wardrobe mirror, Kate's mood had been one of tremulous anticipation. Smiling at him now, she felt nothing but implacable resolve.)

Unconsciously echoing Phil's theme of a few hours earlier, Deiter was talking about Life and How It Let You Down.

'What a bitch,' he complained. 'You shout, march, petition, get beaten up and thrown in jail – but that's fine because you're one of those dickheads who believes justice is worth fighting for. Then one day you wake up to the realization that it's got you nowhere. Mega bucks, political corruption, international right-wing conspiracy and all the rest of it have been in there and done their business. Footsteps in sand. Steam on glass. That's the truth of it. Not a trace, not a mark. Everything's been smoothed over. Like you never did anything, were never there. Know what I mean?'

> Know what I mean?
> It's all been a dream
> No one and nothing
> Is quite what they seem.

Deiter's prow-shaped penis, roughly five inches long when erect, listed like his politics unequivocally to the left. The thin, stretchy skin was the colour of pale parchment and, when retracted, revealed glans of a rosy shade of red. Lying on his back, legs parted, the dark scrotum with its sprinkling of sparse gingery hairs sagged in empty, wrinkled folds towards his anus. Kate absorbed all these particulars with the same heightened awareness she had experienced earlier on the bus. She noticed the feel, shape and cheesy smell. More subliminally, she registered the dynamics of the organ's spatial relationship to the white and bony body of which it was part.

Deiter found this attention to his sexual apparatus highly arousing and was hanging on to control by the skin of his teeth.

'Come on,' he eventually burst out. 'Let's get on with it!'

Actual intercourse lasted less than three minutes. Afterwards they lay in a post-coital drift on the narrow bed that was prettily decked out with a pink nylon counterpane and blue nylon sheets. Above their heads, dangling unevenly on a long flex, a ceiling light glowed through a pink pleated plastic shade. In one corner of the room was a sink with brown streaks smearing the porcelain from taps to plug-hole (like track marks on a boy's dirty underpants, Kate thought). In another stood a flower-sprigged plastic waste-paper bin. There was no wardrobe or chest of drawers, just five coat hooks on a strip of plasticated wood screwed into the wall. All these furnishings were jammed into the six-by-nine cubicle that the Hotel Paradise offered as a single room. For Kate, however, its cramped fakery was the perfect setting for laying her fantasy to rest. There was even a street lamp outside the window casting electric moonbeams into the synthetic dinginess ordained by fate as their lover's bower.

Maria also thought the place was perfect. In silky g-string panties, red spike heels and outrageous uplift bra, she was at that moment dawdling along the wood-patterned lino of the corridor outside (well, who could keep her away?). Pausing by a dusty arrangement of plastic flowers, nostrils quivering delicately at the subversive smell of things damp and unclean, she threw back her head and chuckled throatily. It was a ripe and mellifluous cascade that slid under the door of room 6 and reached Kate as a velvety tickle. With a squirm of delight, Kate opened her mouth and laughed with her.

'What's so funny?'

'Nothing. Just the way things turn out.'

'I'll agree with you there. Tonight has certainly been a surprise, I can tell you!'

Deiter had one hand splayed across the soft flesh of her upper thigh. The other held a litre bottle of duty-free Scotch from which he swigged and dribbled contentedly. His voice was low, relaxed and smooth as fresh putty.

'You know, I really like you,' he confided. 'And I'm not saying that just because you're a good fuck – which you are, I have to admit. No, I get the feeling that what's happened tonight was somehow destined. These things don't happen every day, you know, so we owe it to ourselves to take it further. Explore its potential.'

He paused, took another hefty swig, then gazed at her with innocent confidence. Kate held her breath. Then, just as she began to wonder if he had lost the thread, he came out and actually said it.

'What I'm really getting at is that I'd like you to come to Berlin with me. I want us to spend some real time together.'

Kate crowned herself Queen of the Night.
Triumph (belatedly) was hers.

They were the same words he had spoken seventeen years

ago. She'd been given her cue. Now was her chance to play the scene differently.

'Bugger off,' she said with relish.

'What?'

'You heard.'

Then she jumped out of bed and retrieved Heather's dress from where it lay in a crumpled heap on the floor.

It was 5 a.m.
Night was slip-sliding towards dawn.

The Hotel Paradise was a converted four-storey Victorian terraced house located halfway between Peckham and the Elephant and Castle. A few doors down, announcing itself with an illuminated sign, was a twenty-four hour minicab operation. Kate entered the premises at 5.15 a.m. She carried with her an air of smug satisfaction accentuated by a small, secret smile. Beyond the counter separating the office from the inquiry area two men were drinking tea with their feet stretched towards a Calor gas stove. One of them had a face like an ex-boxer and a paunch so high and round it looked as though he'd stuck a football up his Fair Isle jumper. His companion, tall, good-looking, black, in his forties, was a stylish figure in Levi 501s, leather jacket and suede desert boots.

'Give me a few minutes and I'll be with you,' he said with a faint Caribbean inflection when Kate interrupted their companionable silence to request a car. 'We've had a hard night of it, haven't we, Dave?'

So Kate sat on the bench in the narrow reception area and exchanged a wink with Maria. Maria had covered her nudity with the fur coat Fulvio gave her after she emptied a colander of freshly strained spaghetti into his lap and threatened to leave him. Despite the fact that it had quarterback shoulders and made her look three feet wide, Maria loved the coat and only wore it on special occasions.

'Which is why I've got it on now' she whispered gleefully to Kate. 'I'm so proud of the way you handled that arsehole. And don't think it's just me, either. I can tell you for a fact that every woman who has ever been discounted, disregarded, passed over and forgotten feels exactly as I do.'

This was exactly what Kate wanted to hear. She lit a cigarette and gazed happily at the curls of smoke that floated fancifully towards the ceiling.

'Is that so?' she murmured. 'Tell me more.'

So Maria fished out her contraband Marlboros, crossed her legs and began enthusiastically developing the theme. At the height of her eloquence, however, she was interrupted by the driver who had finished his tea and was beckoning Kate to follow him outside.

'Time to hit the road,' he said cheerfully, zipping up his jacket. 'That's my vehicle over there.'

The car was a down-at-heel Ford family saloon with none of the style of its owner. In fact, when Kate climbed in the smell of disinfectant was so powerful she instinctively recoiled.

'Sorry about the odour,' the driver apologized, rolling down his window and advising her to do the same. 'I've had two drunks spewing up in here tonight. And one right after the other, too. The second was a poor old duffer whose wife just upped and left him after forty years. I couldn't help but feel sorry for him. It pulled the rug from under his feet. I mean, it's hard when things you've always taken for certainties are suddenly certain no more. You know, when you come up against the random or unforeseen.'

The truth of this remark was brought home five minutes

into the journey when they came across a nasty accident. A van and a motor bike had collided at a deserted junction and a young man pumping blood from a gashed leg was lying unconscious in the road. Two ambulancemen on their knees beside him were administering first aid. A few yards away police questioned the shocked and bewildered van driver.

It was a chilling scene and staring at it Kate's sense of well-being evaporated. Her mind filled with beating wings of fear narrowing everything down to her own nerve-centre of dread. Which meant, of course, it was Lorenzo she saw lying there. Lorenzo's overturned and twisted bike. Lorenzo's vulnerable mortality. But just as she was about to give herself over to full-blown panic, she was distracted by a low, rhythmical murmuring coming from the seat in front. It was a controlled but powerful sound and its vibrations had a strangely steadying effect.

'Are you praying?' she asked (actually wondering if he was doing some sort of voodoo).

'Not exactly,' the driver answered. 'I'm chanting for that young man and his recovery. I'm a Buddhist, you see.'

The injured motorcyclist was gently lifted on to a stretcher. A policewoman walked towards them and with wheeling gestures waved them on.

'Going back to what we were saying earlier about things random and unforseen,' he continued, as with sober caution they resumed the journey to north London. 'Those two had the road to themselves and yet they somehow managed to smash right into each other. As a Buddhist, I believe it happened because of their karma.'

'Drink or drugs more likely,' said Kate, rejecting this as far too superstitious and fatalistic.

The driver grinned. 'Ah, but you see karma is just another word for cause and effect, so getting tanked up or high is part of the whole caboodle. I'll try and explain it to you.'

And he did.
As they cruised the dark and empty streets.
It was like being at a lecture.

'OK,' he began. 'First, Buddhism says life is eternal – that's to say we're born, we die, we're born again, we die again and so on for ever. Secondly, karma is created in three ways: what we think, what we say, what we do. The karma we're born with is the karma we've created by our actions in our past lives. Old karma is manifested in the way we look, the parents we've got, our natural talents, basic personality and so on. After that we continue to create new karma every day with our thoughts, words and deeds. With me so far?

'Now take that young chap back there. Let's say his past karma meant he was born with an angry and aggressive nature. And suppose he had a row with his girlfriend tonight. Another person might have called up a mate, done some soul-searching, slept on it or whatever. But his angry nature determined that he'd choose an angry outlet – which might mean getting rat-arsed and driving like a maniac. To sum up, his angry life state, formed by past karma, resulted in a negative cause; getting drunk. And the effect of that cause was an accident. Get it?'

'But what if he was stone-cold sober and on his way to work? What if he took a last-minute detour and got hit when the van skidded on a patch of oil? That would be chance, nothing else.'

'Buddhism says there's no such thing as chance. Just different karma and a different sequence of cause and effect. Cause and effect determines everything. Why anyone is anywhere doing anything at any given time.'

'Like you and me in this car now?'

The driver grinned again, 'Of course.'

The fare came to eight pounds. Kate was so enthralled by the conversation she added a two-pound tip. By now the sky was lightening, enough for her to spot Mad Max strolling towards them down the street.

'See that cat,' she said, pointing him out. 'Well, I'm pretty sure he and I have been acquainted in some other dimension.'

'Is he yours?'

'No. We're just friends.'

'Friends are very precious.'

'I think so too.'

There was a pause, then by unspoken agreement they shook hands.

'My name's Owen, by the way. What's yours?'

'Kate.'

'Nice speaking with you Kate. You look after yourself, you hear?'

Chapter 19

Another thing Owen said was:

To understand the present look at the causes you made in the past. To know the future look at the causes you are making now.

Which Kate found profound but also a little disturbing. It cast an uneasy light on the sequence of events that made up her own life, not to mention everyone else's. It certainly made her ponder the karmic significance of an item she had come across in yesterday's evening paper. So much so, in fact, that she insisted on sharing it with Sadie, who had turned up unexpectedly on the doorstep. With solemn emphasis she read:
 'Boy Sees Father Die at Graveside. Eight months after losing his mother to alcoholic poisoning, eight-year-old Billy watched helplessly as lightning struck his father and killed him during a visit to her grave at a Baltimore cemetery. Robert White, 41, had just finished placing a red rose on the grave when a lightning bolt hit the tree under which they were sheltering. It first split the tree and then struck Mr White, apparently hitting him on a St Christopher's medal hanging around his neck.'
 Sadie listened with the same irritated expression with which she had endured Kate's awed recital of Owen's various enlightened utterances. 'Let's get this straight,'

she snapped when Kate had finished. 'Your minicab guru is saying that it's all down to us, right? Forget chance, bad luck, mishaps, acts of God or whatever. We shape our miserable lives with every breath we take. Well, I've heard that esoteric stuff before and I don't buy it. And just for the record, sweetie, I've done time on an ashram too, you know!'

Sadie was not in a good mood. Furthermore, she was certainly not interested in any philosophy that took a hard line on personal responsibility. Since Pete's birthday bash – which cost her all of 'two-fucking-grand' – she had been on a mega down, and the sole reason for her visit was to indulge in a session of blame and bitterness. Not that she had anything new to say. Pete was a lazy, sponging and irresponsible oaf. Jasmine was a fourteen-and-a-half-year-old renegade who chewed gum, ate her bogies, stole money, borrowed and criminally ruined Sadie's expensive clothes. (Her most serious fault, however, which never got mentioned, was being a slim, waifish elf whose luminous beauty reminded her mother of the glory she had lost.) Together, Sadie declared, these two blood-sucking parasites were sabotaging her chance of happiness. Big time.

'Ah, but what *is* happiness exactly?' Kate interrupted, still eager for metaphysical debate. 'I mean, isn't it part of the problem that we just don't know?'

But Sadie would not be drawn. 'Listen, dum-dum,' she said shortly. 'Happiness is getting what you want, when you want and in bloody great shovelfuls. OK?'

Which was one way of looking at it, after all.

By then it was twelve-fifteen and Kate had been awake for almost thirty hours. She had been pleased enough to see her friend, but now she wanted her to go. She longed for a hot bath and an uninterrupted siesta – in that order. But this, it seemed, was not to be. The pursuit of happiness (Sadie-style) had moved to the top of the day's agenda. And Sadie's idea of happiness – in its immediate form, at least – was to go to her favourite Covent Garden café where the *crème brûlée* was 'simply divine'. Kate was appalled.

'You must be joking.'

'Why should I be joking?'

'I'm too tired.'

'You might be tired, but I'm suicidally depressed.'

'Frankly I don't care if you top yourself. I want to go to bed.'

They glowered at each other over a choppy divide. For the first time since their renewed acquaintance conflict was threatening. Sadie's breath whistled sharply through the pearly barricade of her expensively capped teeth.

'Cause and effect! Karmic retribution! Lack of compassion!' she hissed, stabbing her smouldering cigarette in Kate's direction. 'Just think about that!'

The café was on the corner of the market facing St Paul's church. Large rectangular umbrellas like starched linen napkins protected the alfresco tables from a gunmetal sky. In the piazza between the church and the café a performer in oversized check trousers and face paint was entertaining a handful of out-of-season tourists with a comic routine. Sadie's humour – as befits a devotee of instant gratification – was now fully restored.

'Isn't this nice?' she crooned through a creamy mouthful of custard and caramelized sugar. 'Just hanging out and watching people? I mean, this is what life's like in Rome and Paris and anywhere else that's halfway decent. And don't let anyone tell you it's the weather that keeps the

British closeted indoors. It's merely that we're anal retentive.'

Kate, furious with herself for being there, did not reply. Not that her resentful silence bothered Sadie, who proceeded to expound the theory that schools like Eton put something in the food that permanently reduced the boys' testosterone levels. Mid-monologue, however, her attention was diverted. The golden eyes widened and she jabbed Kate sharply in the ribs.

'Wow!' she breathed. 'Now is that a bum or isn't it!'

Kate turned her head reluctantly in the direction indicated and was presented with the sight of a well-formed backside clad in black lycra cycling shorts. It belonged to a strapping young lad standing with his back to them, consulting an A-Z.

After a minute or so he tucked the book under his arm and strolled off. The muscular nates bunching and relaxing to the rhythm of his rolling gait were a pleasure to behold.

It was only when he moved off, however, unblocking the view of two women with shaven heads seated a few tables down to their left, that Kate's interest became truly engaged. As it so happened one of the women was wearing a top made from the same black lycra as the cycling shorts. Cut like a vest, and worn under an unzipped leather biker's jacket, the stretchy material defined the twin spheres of her chest as neatly as it had the young man's rear. But there the comparison ended. For unlike the well-rounded, orbicular cheeks, these protuberances were small and distinctly flat.

Like collapsed meringues.
Like mud pies subsiding back into sludge.

The reason Kate stared so hard was not just that breasts – hers and everyone else's – were an eternal obsession. It was the uncomfortable tickle, the stirring of a reluctant memory, that the sight of them provoked. Unenticing and unexceptional though they were, they caught and held her eyes with the tenacity of fish-hooks. At first she was confused by their mesmerizing power. Then realization dawned.

Somewhere, somehow, sometime she had seen those tits before!

The intensity of her scrutiny made itself felt. The woman removed her Rayban Wayfarers and, squinting short-sightedly, returned the stare. Then she sprang to her feet and shrieked. It was the sound that did it. That piercing reverberation last heard teetering on the edge of hysteria as Daniele dragged her into the lift. The shaven head identified itself as blonde stubble, the features composed themselves into a recognizable fit.

'Who the fuck's that?' Sadie exclaimed in some alarm as the woman lunged towards them and clasped Kate in an emotional embrace.

Kate put up with the laughing, crying and rib-bruising for a few short moments, then pushed her away. 'Sadie,' she said coolly. 'Meet Louisa, my estranged husband's ex.'

As it turned out, the Louisa Kate was now confronting was a very different woman from the one she had known. For when the dust finally settled, she emerged phoenix-like from her involvement with Daniele as an ardent lover of her own sex. Which really suited her. For the discovery of her Sapphic libido tapped into the most generous and uncritical part of her nature. She now embraced all womankind with unreserved love and respect. Specifically, however, the focus of her ardour was the other bald-headed woman now following Louisa to join them at their table.

Carla was short, slight, self-possessed and in her early twenties. She had close-set brown eyes, a patrician nose and a large, dark mole nestling like a furry dimple in the centre of her chin. Despite the lack of hair this highly distinctive feature allowed Kate to recognize her almost immediately. And when she did it was all she could do not to laugh. For Carla was none other than the adored only child of a man Kate had always disliked – the rich, powerful and manipulative editor of Daniele and Louisa's newspaper.

The first time Kate met her she was dressed like a sugar-plum fairy in flounces of pink organza. The occasion was her tenth birthday party to which Lorenzo, along with offspring of other newspaper employees, had been invited. After gorging on chocolate and ice-cream, the children were entertained by a magician sporting a sequined waistcoat and spectacular, four-inch-high quiff. For his finale he produced a dove which flew towards the ceiling and plucked from thin air a gold chain studded with tiny rubies. At this point the birthday girl was led to the front of the audience by her father. There he went down on his knees and fastened the trinket around her thin little neck.

'From Mamma and Papa,' he intoned with embarrassing reverence. 'To brighten the smile of our precious princess.'

It didn't brighten her smile, of course. A few minutes later she threw an awesome tantrum and was dragged away by her au pair in floods of tears and snot.

Thereafter contact with P.P. (Precious Princess) was restricted to the odd sighting. On one occasion Kate spotted her scowling out of her father's office with a painful crop of teenage acne. On another she was chaining an expensive new Lambretta to railings near Lorenzo's school. The last time was three or four years previously outside MacDonald's in the Piazza di Spagna. She was smoking, eating a hamburger and French-kissing a youth wearing flash Mexican riding boots – all at the same time. (The reason Kate retained this scene was because Carla squeezed her Big Mac so passionately ketchup spurted down the back of his shirt.)

Now it seemed that their personal ley-lines had drawn them to this more meaningful intersection – not that Carla was aware of it for, like Deiter, she had no recollection of having met Kate before. Just as Kate was about to remind her, however (with fond recollections of her birthday tantrum), Carla spoke first.

'I've been told all the chic dykes go to the Hot Cleft on Tuesdays,' she said, her thick Italian accent overlaid with a fashionable cockney twang. 'Have you checked it out?'

'The Hot Cleft? Kate?' Louisa shrieked, bursting into hilarious giggles. 'You must be joking! Nothing could be more unlikely!'

The fact that Carla automatically assumed she was a lesbian gave Kate a shock (I mean, did she look like one, for God's sake?). Now, however, she was more outraged that Louisa should think she was so stuck in her groove, so incapable of making changes, that the idea of her and Hot Cleft was a screaming joke. Indeed, she was so inflamed she determined to prove otherwise. And if that meant following them to some gay club, then so be it.

She'd show the cow!

So at three-fifty, therefore, when they left the café to drink Bloody Marys and Guinness at a nearby pub, Kate went with them. At seven they caught a cab to Carla's favourite Greek restaurant situated behind Centre Point. (By now they were all aware that she had lived for eight months in Palmer's Green and knew the city better than any of them). 'Trust me,' she said, when Louisa mentioned preferring

Chinese. 'This place is good, cheap and frequented by celebrities.'

They were not disappointed. For eight pounds fifty a head, excluding the retsina, they worked their way through a menu of succulent starters, lamb stewed with tomatoes and honey-drenched baklavas. (There was also a celebrity in the person of a famous TV comic.) Sadie – whose appetite was unaffected by the *crème brûlée*, crisps and beer – ate for England. Louisa and Carla watched her with admiration. 'You're so beautiful!' they exclaimed. 'So life-enhancing! And such magnificent eyes!'

Sadie was having a great time and these compliments, together with the retsina, fuelled her euphoric abandon. 'I want to dance, sing and go crazy,' she proclaimed, cheeks crimson and flesh quivering. 'I want to be wild, wild, wild!'

This outburst sent a *frisson* around the table. Even Kate, who was still annoyed with Sadie, felt herself responding.

On leaving the restaurant Carla walked straight into the arms of a friend who had once been a traffic warden but now had a stall in Camden market.

'Forget clubbing,' she insisted. 'I'm going to a party. You must all come too.'

There was a brief debate during which Kate seized the opportunity to show Louisa her ability to be unpredictable and free. 'Suits me,' she said. 'In fact, it sounds like fun.'

The party was in Camden Town, on a labyrinthine council estate consisting of ramps, stairways, underpasses and blustery walkways. Nix – their hostess and also a market trader (candles, crystals, incense, etcetera) – opened the door to them wearing a black rubber bustier and matching mini so short it gave glimpses of the black rubber knickers underneath.

'Welcome ladies,' she said in delight. 'The food's run out but the drink and drugs haven't.'

Despite appearances Nix was not a fetishist – although

she certainly got a kick out of dressing up. Business had been bad for two years and she was considering doing rubber gear instead. Before taking the final plunge, however, she was doing some market research. Her main purpose for wearing this sample outfit was to get the reaction of her guests. Which included Kate.

'Well, darling?' she demanded, pivoting elegantly on thigh-high, black patent boots. 'What do you think? Over the top, eh? But this is for fun, for partying. When I get going I intend doing everything from jeans and hot pants to sedate little dresses you could wear to the office. In fact, I want to take rubber out of the closet and into mainstream fashion.'

'Great idea,' Kate replied, still bent on changing Louisa's idea of her. 'In fact, I can imagine wearing rubber jeans myself.'

'There you are!' Nix rejoined enthusiastically. 'My message is that rubber's for everyone. Even for a big woman like that one over there.'

Kate thought she was referring to Sadie. Instead she turned to see Phil, still wearing her baggy green overalls, weaving her way towards her through the festive crush.

'Well, is this a small world or what?' she boomed, clapping a large hand on Kate's shoulder. 'You didn't mention having market connections.'

'I haven't. I'm with some friends.

And at that instant Carla materialized at her elbow. So she introduced them.

Kate did not believe in love at first sight and never had done. Now, however, she saw it happen before her very eyes.

'Phil?' Carla repeated (pronouncing it 'Feel') in a lilting, breathless whisper. 'What a beautiful name.' Then, gazing up into the plain, good-natured face with an expression of total wonderment, she murmured, 'Phil, you cannot know how happy I am to meet you.'

But it was obvious from the reflected awe on Phil's face that she did. She understood immediately this had nothing to do with Latin exaggeration but came straight from Carla's heart.

And forty-five minutes later – after Louisa found them embracing passionately on the narrow kitchen balcony – everyone else knew it, too.

Chapter 20

It must be stressed that Phil and Carla were not simply responding to sexual attraction with a reckless and impromptu snog. They were responding to Destiny which, as everyone knows, is a Law Unto Itself. Louisa was not aware of this, of course, and consequently all she saw was filthy and cruel betrayal. So with a chilling howl she leapt on Carla's back and savagely wrenched her from Phil's arms.

Until this moment Phil and Carla had been in seventh heaven. It flushed their cheeks, glazed their eyes and filled their ears with the song of angels. It also turned their tongues into semi-paralysed gastropods that heaved and flopped ineffectually as they tried to explain themselves. The words stumbled out in clumsy bundles, arranging themselves into phrases such as: 'You mustn't take this personally!' 'It was a bolt from the blue!' 'It was meant to be!' 'Our love can't be denied!' And so on. They should have known, of course, that it was wasted effort. Louisa couldn't – or wouldn't – understand what they were saying.

So with helpless shrugs they made a hasty getaway. In the refreshments van.

Their departure was the signal for Nix and other females to rally round. Louisa's glass was refilled, a bog roll was produced and solidarity was demonstrated with personal testimonies of similar cruel betrayal. After a while, however, the blubbing became tedious, so they rejoined the party and let her get on with it. Music, laughter and unconcern washed over her hunched shoulders and bowed, shaven head like water over the prow of a sinking ship. And as she disappeared beneath the bright surface of collective revelry, people simply forgot she was there.

Except for Kate, that is. She peered into the pitching chasm and with a death's-head grin followed her ex-rival's plunge into misery. She saw the heart break, the blood spill and the fragments of mashed bone fly everywhere. She wasn't a cruel woman, but there was much satisfaction in witnessing Louisa getting her just deserts. But then, sounding high above the general racket, came a hiccupping cascade of drunken giggles – unmistakably Sadie's. For some reason the instant hostility this sound aroused snapped Kate's humour from vindictive pleasure to something resembling pity.

'Where are you staying?' she asked in a brusque (but not unkind) tone. 'Shall I get Nix to call you a cab?'

Louisa raised her head, shell-shocked and blank. 'A cab?' she whimpered. 'I don't want a cab. I want to die!'

At which point Kate made the reluctant decision to take her home. After all, who wants a suicide on their conscience?

Heather's flat was dismal at the best of times. At that hour, with night pressing damply against the windows, it was particularly so. The air felt dense and compacted, as though being sandwiched between the clay soil beneath the floorboards and the slumbering weight of the house above was squeezing it of all oxygen. Kate, however, was not feeling oppressed. On the contrary, making coffee in the small kitchen she experienced a surge of the fizzy energy again.

Louisa too was remarkably revived. She sat at the table unpacking the contents of her black leather rucksack, which (a tribute to efficient travelling) contained everything she needed for her stay: four pairs of black silk knickers, two pairs of thirty-denier black lycra tights, two T-shirts, a black lycra miniskirt, a black Max Mara roll-neck sweater, make-up and toiletries. She also pulled out a Nikon camera, a flash gun and six rolls of black and white film.

Louisa had not come to London for a romantic interlude. Indeed, as she now told Kate, Carla's decision to accompany her had been made at the last minute. The purpose of her visit was to photograph Gertrude Maud Baker, an eighty-seven-year-old artist who was 'absolutely brilliant and the angriest person in the world'.

'Why is she so angry?' Kate asked.

'Because her father married the nursemaid after her mother's death when she was twelve. She loved him with an incestuous passion, you see, and the rage she felt at his betrayal has never diminished. You have to see it to believe it. She's a deranged adolescent inhabiting an old woman's body.'

Talking about betrayal started the rivers streaming from her eyes again. She gulped down the coffee Kate gave her and let the salty tears vaporize in an upsurge of aromatic steam.

'When are you seeing her?'

'Ten a.m. tomorrow. I mean, today,' Louisa fumbled for the bog roll (which she'd hung on to) and gave her nose a loud blow. 'In fact, I'd be really grateful if you'd come with me. I feel too wrecked to face her alone.'

There was a brief pause, during which Kate reflected wonderingly at her benevolence to the cow responsible –

technically, at least – for the break-up of her marriage. Admiring self-approval and admiration almost overwhelmed her. Her entire being was flooded with a warm glow.

'Will you? Please?'

The smile Kate gave her was genuine. 'Of course,' she said, graciously. 'In fact, I'd like to.'

By then it was four-thirty.
She had been awake for forty-seven hours.

That Louisa had not exaggerated her description of Gertrude Maud Baker (whom she'd met two years earlier when the artist visited Rome) was made clear when they arrived for the appointment. 'Oh, God, I'd forgotten you were coming,' said Tristan, her pony-tailed young assistant when he opened the door. 'Look, we're having a bit of a problem. The demons were with her when she got up this morning and she's destroyed a piece she's been working on for a month. I'm afraid you'll have to wait here until things have settled a bit.'

'Here' was the bottom of a wide flight of uncarpeted stairs. From this position Kate and Louisa could survey the open-plan ground floor which was littered with piles of bricks and bags of cement. In fact, it looked like a building site. To pass the time Louisa filled her in with more of Gertrude's story. 'She moved here on 20 September 1946. The very next day she redefined the ground-floor space by demolishing the wall between the entrance hall and the front room with a sledgehammer. Since then the house has existed in a state of DIY flux. Walls have come down, banisters have been jettisoned, doors boarded up, new windows created. Even the kitchen has been relocated four times. She does all the work herself, but nothing is ever finished.'

'Why doesn't she call in professionals?'

'Because her living environment is a manifestation of her inner state, that's why,' Louisa said, dropping her voice to a whisper. 'To someone like her a normal house would be a source of impossible disharmony. I know because I've read everything that's ever been written about her. She's my greatest heroine.'

Forty minutes later Tristan returned and took them up to the first-floor studio. Gertrude, wearing a blue cardigan and shapeless grey skirt, was standing in the centre of the room. Her small, wiry frame with its pronounced widow's hump was vibrating with unspent fury.

'So what are you here for?' She screeched as they entered. 'If you think I'm going to let you exploit and manipulate me with your camera, you're mistaken! I'm sick of it! I'm sick of vandals like you breaking into my life and carting chunks of it away!'

Just as they were about to turn tail and run, however, she suddenly abandoned her attack. The reason for this was that she had become transfixed by the grief-ridden awfulness of Louisa's face (the devastation accentuated by make-up slapped on in the taxi coming over). Drawing closer, she peered intently at the bloodshot, ping-pong ball eyes, the nose so swollen Louisa was obliged to breathe through her mouth, the red puffiness of the tear-sodden flesh. Clucking her approval, she followed the sorrowful contours from bald head to trembling chin with a calloused and arthritic finger. And by the time she had finished her inspection her mood had changed. 'I'm going to the basement to do some welding,' she informed Louisa sweetly. 'You can take pictures of me there.'

'Thank God for that,' said Tristan when they'd gone.

'Louisa told me she can be temperamental.'

'To put it mildly. Do you know her work?'

Vida Adamoli

Kate shook her head. 'To tell the truth, I'd never heard of her until today.'

'That's understandable. She's ignored by the art establishment and it's a nightmare trying to persuade her to have a show. Her last one was eight years ago in Berlin.'

'What's this?' Kate walked over to a large square box the size of a large Wendy house.

'It's called "That Kiss 4",' Tristan followed her and pulled aside the curtain of dark red velvet hanging across the opening. 'Take a look.'

The inside of the box was entirely covered in the same dark red velvet as the curtain. Underneath the velvet, billowing out of the walls and ceiling, were cushioned protuberances shaped like huge lips and tongues which nudged Kate obscenely as she pressed into the confined space. After a minute or so, crouched on the velvet floor and enveloped in voluptuous redness, she became aware of the sound of two people breathing. Soft at first, so soft she had to strain to hear it, the sounds were amplified until they became an urgent, gasping duet. And then a thin cry of protest joined the reverberations. A piercing note of desperation that froze the heart.

'All Gertrude's work is an attempt to deal with her memories. She's not interested in anything else,' Tristan explained when Kate stumbled out. 'Once she's recreated a moment, pinned it down, so to speak, then she can let it go with a measure of peace. Not that it works with the really big themes. She's driven back to those over and over again. This installation is one of four and it focuses on the feelings she had when she hid behind the drawing-room curtains and saw her father and her nursemaid kissing. The others are over here.'

He led her to three boxes two-foot square mounted on the wall. Peering into 'That Kiss 1', Kate saw a small painting of a deserted entrance hall viewed from the top of a flight of stairs. 'That Kiss 2' showed a looming panelled door with a flower-patterned, white china handle. 'That Kiss 3' was simply a painting of red velvet curtains draped in heavy folds across a bay window.

There was one other structure in the studio. Three metal rods had been welded to form a wide pyramid over a white block. Set on the block were the casts of two feet with their soles pressed tightly together. One foot was small and crabbed with a puffy fold of skin around the ankle. The other was elongated and bony and the long, flexible toes curled to hold the smaller ones in a protective embrace. 'Gertrude's foot and mine. It's a portrait of our relationship. You'll notice that although the piece is placed within a circumscribed space, it's immediately accessible. It's only pain she has to box in.' He stared at it intensely for a moment, then roused himself. 'But that's enough for now. Let me show you the garden.'

They went back down the stairs, past the bricks and bags of cement, out through French windows and into a delightful jungle. Huge clumps of bamboo loomed over a path overgrown with ivy, and everywhere fierce rose-bushes that had never known pruning shears forced their thorny ramifications through rampant tangles of evergreen foliage. There was also a pond with water lilies and goldfish the size of toy submarines. Gazing down at them Kate was drawn into a memory box of her own. The pond became the glass fruit bowl where Batman and Robin, the two goldfish Lorenzo had won at a fair, shared a habitat with a sprig of plastic seaweed and a few shells. 'The poor kid only had them for three days,' she told Tristan. 'On the fourth he found them floating belly up.'

'Belly up, eh?' echoed Tristan in such a sombre tone that Kate glanced round. It was then that she noticed the smattering of small purple sores on his face. And he noticed her noticing. 'Kaposi's sarcoma,' he said. 'You get

Vida Adamoli

it with Aids.' Then he threw back his head and laughed.

    'Birth, and copulation, and death
    That's all the facts when you come to brass tacks.

'Keats,' he explained gently.

Chapter 21

Many times during the last two sleep-deprived days Kate had experienced a breakdown of normal functioning. Her body alternated between feeling numb and disconnected and tingling rushes, as though Alka Seltzer had been injected into her veins. It was the same with her mind. One moment it was sharp and receptive, the next an empty space echoing with muffled and incomprehensible sounds. At two-thirty that afternoon, after a marathon fifty-seven hours of wakefulness, she finally got to bed. It was like falling into an ether-filled vortex and she was only halfway across the room when unconsciousness rushed up to claim her. Her muscles became paralysed, her dream-starved brain went into immediate hallucinatory action, and she was out for the count when Louisa crawled under the duvet beside her.

For the next two days she was lost to the picture-world of sleep, the familiar land of cryptic charades and quicksand stage sets that dissolved and re-formed at each successive flick of a surreal brain switch. In a procession of disembodied and unrestrained encounters she talked, laughed, argued and erotically dallied with both the living and the dead. She glided through deserted streets in Owen's minicab and soared in ecstatic flight over trees whose topmost branches reached up to brush her belly. At the end of her journey she was welcomed to a house by a group of people who had long been awaiting her return.

'Sum-Yu!' they exclaimed, gathering round her.

'Sum-Yu?' said Kate with a puzzled frown. Then she looked in a mirror and saw not herself but an elderly Chinese gentleman. As she stood staring, Lidia appeared reflected in the glass beside her.

'Sum-of-You,' she explained, stressing each syllable with a patient smile.

'Sum-of-*Me*?' repeated Kate, awed.

And, mumbling these words, she awoke.

Earlier that morning, before leaving to catch her plane, Louisa had scribbled a note which she placed under the salt-cellar on the kitchen table. It read: *Tried to say goodbye but couldn't rouse you. You looked horribly waxen – I hope you're not dead!*

Kate read the note several times before the words made any sense. For although she was not dead, she wasn't all that alive either. Her long period of unconsciousness had left her feeling like a zombie. Her brain was coated with a thick growth of sleep-mould and her five faculties, saturated with the poppied spore, were having a hard time making sense of her surroundings. It took several minutes of empty contemplation of a toothbrush, for example, to work out what she was holding it for.

When Sean arrived around lunch-time she was still out of it – although he was too preoccupied with his own troubles to notice. He flung himself face down on the sofa where he had passed so many bloated hours and sobbed unashamedly into the upholstery. The reason for his distress was Phil's departure. 'She's gone!' he wept. 'Gone with that ugly Eyetie to live in Rome. Not only has my mother become a lesbian, but the creature she's run off with is at least four years younger than me! But does the unnatural bitch give a damn about the trauma she's putting me through? Not a bit of it! She thinks I'm lucky she's left me the refreshment van!'

The words 'unnatural bitch' made an impact on Kate's unfocused mind. She realized she was not responding true to her maternal type. Or, to put it another way, Sean's distress touched her not in the slightest.

'Well?' he said, as her silence began to impinge.

'Well what?'

'Well, what do you say?'

'What can I say?'

'Something. Surely you can say something!'

It was a reasonable request and she squeezed her temples in an effort to concentrate. 'Life's a curious and unpredictable affair,' she offered eventually.

Which was the best she could do.
In the circumstances.

Sean departed, leaving the forlorn imprint of his tears on the sofa. Outside rain drizzled softly. Discovering that he had smoked the last of her cigarettes, Kate took the broken umbrella kept propped by the front door and went to the corner shop. The Indian proprietor was watching a video of a Hindi love story on the small TV installed under the counter. It was clearly an affecting romance because his eyes were swimming as he handed over her change. At which point Kate decided that life was not only curious and unpredictable. Of late it had also been pretty waterlogged.

Back at the flat, stretched out in front of the gas fire, her mind slid into neutral again. In a meandering, unstructured way her thoughts drifted to Louisa and Phil and Carla and Sadie. And on to Heather and Maria and Lidia and her mother and all the other women she had ever known. It occurred to her that Lidia and Gertrude were about the same age. What would Glorious Talent and Glorious Widowhood make of each other, she wondered?

Thinking about Gertrude led to a musing on pain and how useful it would be to put some of her own into a box. She imagined sticking select, palpitating bits into jamjars and lining them up like interesting specimens in a medical laboratory. She would label them: *Hello Marital Infidelity. Goodbye Wondrous Breasts. So Long Darling Child. Enter Vortex. Exit Self.*

And so on and so forth.

Her thoughts moved on. This time to Tristan and the purple stigmata of his impending death. They came to her now as wine stains spotting a fresh white tablecloth. As evil hieroglyphics telling the *cognoscente* that the main course of the feast would never be served. Closing her eyes, she saw Tristan and Gertrude waltzing slowly up and down the long studio beneath bright lights fixed in a straight line to tracks down the centre of the ceiling. A love dance. A death dance. A spectral spin along the road to their graves.

And then the phone rang.

'*Pronto*? Mamma?'

'Lorenzo!' Instinctive joy followed by the usual leap of anxiety. 'Are you all right?'

'Of course I'm all right. I just wanted to wish you happy birthday.'

'Happy birthday?'

'*Porco dio*, you're senile already! It's the fifteenth of November, in case you've forgotten.'

'Of course not,' she lied. 'What news, darling?'

'Nothing much. Except Dad says to tell you he's got gallstones and he's pissing blood. He also says he won't get you a present until you stop being an idiot and come home.'

'What's he got in mind? Diamond-studded rubber gloves?'

'Listen, it's no joke. Yesterday he dragged me over to cook pasta and *fagioli* and then complained it didn't taste like yours.'

'Isn't Lidia feeding him?'

'*Nonna*'s had enough. She told him he was the architect of his own misfortune. Anyway, she's gone on a six-week cruise to the Maldives with Signora Pina.'

'Good for her,' said Kate, smiling. 'I hope she took a bikini.'

This frivolous response did not go down well with her darling angel. So for the next ten minutes she dedicated herself to giving sympathetic encouragement – along with a foolproof recipe for his father's favourite soup. They both agreed Daniele was a pain in the arse, and when the time came to say goodbye Kate felt she had redeemed herself. As she put down the phone it rang again immediately. This time it was her mother in Tel Aviv.

'Forty-one years old and spending your birthday alone in a grubby basement. Not exactly a happy situation, is it?'

'It's not that bad.'

'Not that bad! What could be worse, for God's sake?'

'If you want I can tell you.'

'Listen, darling, I'm just concerned about you. We all are. In fact, Daniele and I had a long conversation about you just the other day. Are you interested in hearing what your husband has to say?'

Kate gave an exasperated sigh. 'I know what my

husband has to say, Mother. My husband says he's got gallstones.'

By the time her mother rang off it was getting dark. Instead of switching on the lights, Kate settled back to watch the seeping twilight fill the room with softness. It was like the early days. Back on her island again, herself with herself, herself within herself. An appropriate place for coming to terms with the fact that her forty-first birthday had sneaked up on her while she was temporarily distracted.

She was not distracted now, though. On the contrary, she had regained full consciousness and was ready to give herself some quality-time attention.

'So, who's the lucky birthday girl?' she crooned sweetly. 'Forty-one years old and on course for fifty!' She slopped imaginary champagne into an imaginary glass and raised it in a toast. 'Here's to Kate . . .' she began, then stopped as her dream suddenly came flooding back to her. 'No. Let's do that again. Here's to Sum-Yu and a Sum-Of-You future!'

Which sounded much better.

Chapter 22

It was almost ten years since Kate's mother married her gynaecologist and went to live in Israel. Kate spent the fraught week prior to her departure helping with last-minute packing, after which contact with her childhood home was severed. She revisited it in dreams, of course, and occasionally in fantasy while awake. When she did it was not fun. Images of its pebble-dashed, suburban neatness crawling like the end-segment of a brick caterpillar over the soft rise of the road revived feelings of unhappiness and alienation, and little else.

It was back to her father's dislike of and hostility towards her adolescent metamorphosis/the tension of her mother's repressed yearnings/the oceans of tears shed in the comfortless privacy of her pretty pink bedroom/the hours spent moping in the sterile crazy-paved garden, as marooned as the stiffly pruned roses in their diamond cut-outs of stony earth.

No nostalgic mileage to be had there!

In the gathering darkness of Heather's sitting room, however, celebrating her birthday and Sum-of-You future with make-believe champagne, she acknowledged that to go forward one had first to go back. Something important of herself was trapped in that semi-detached past. The time had come to listen to its voice, she decided, and mount a rescue.

'When?' Maria, Heather and Lidia demanded in unison.

'Tomorrow,' Kate said resolutely. 'First thing.'

'First thing' ended up being mid-afternoon (reluctance surfaced at breakfast and clamped on the irons). When she eventually got there, dragging her feet past clipped privets and long lines of immaculately maintained cars, she found the house somewhat changed. A wrought-iron gate with the number 9 incorporated into the design had replaced the old wooden one. Grecian-style stone urns planted with begonias, petunias and trailing lobelia stood on square pedestals either side of the front porch (now boxed in with frosted glass). The brickwork on the lower half of the facade had been painted tile red, and in the bay window a china troika driven by a maiden with streaming hair galloped past snowy drifts of white net. There was also a large For Sale sign affixed to the fence. While she was staring up at it a grey Ford Siesta drew up at the kerb and a woman in her late fifties got out.

'Hello,' she said. 'Mrs Anderson? I hope you haven't been waiting long. The man from the estate agent said five.'

'Actually, I'm not Mrs Anderson. And I haven't come from the estate agent's,' Kate was apologetic. 'I'd really like to see the house, though. Would that be possible?'

The woman hesitated. Her arms were full of groceries and polythene-wrapped clothes from the dry-cleaner's. As she turned to lock the car door one of the garments slithered from her grasp. Kate, anxious to ingratiate herself, swiftly retrieved it.

'Well, as you can see from the sign, viewing is by appointment only. Still,' she conceded reluctantly, 'you're here now so I suppose you'd better come in.'

Kate smiled, murmured her thanks and, taking a deep

breath, followed her inside. Stepping gingerly over the threshold she heard a loud crash as a whole decade dropped away behind her. 'Whoops!' she exclaimed, stumbling over the doormat. Then she looked up and was confronted by her own face staring out of a gilt-framed mirror on the opposite wall. To meet herself so soon was unnerving (to say the least) and for a moment she stood transfixed.

'I see you've noticed the mirror,' the woman said, interpreting this seizure as admiration. 'I fell in love with it at first sight, too. It's genuine Victorian, of course, not reproduction. You can always tell.'

The mirror was repro, as it happened, and also quite cheap. Kate knew this because she had been with her mother when she bought it and it was one of the items sold along with the house. Another was the repro Jacobean rug chest still occupying the same position left of the front door. While Mrs Greenberg (as she now introduced herself) unloaded the shopping in the kitchen, Kate drew closer to trace the familiar patterns carved into the surface. Skimming the grooves and ridges made her fingertips tingle. She could feel the reverberations of her mother's thousands of hours of feverish polishing rising through the layers of impacted wax. At the same time she became aware of a charged undercurrent, like the build-up of atmospheric pressure preceding a storm. *So they're all still here*, she thought with a shiver of anticipation. All the old thoughts, feelings and wounded energy.

Waiting.

When Kate decided on the rescue she envisaged it as a hit-and-run job. She expected to come across herself huddled in some particularly painful corner, a convenient location from which she could pluck herself to safety. Not so. As she discovered, trailing Mrs Greenberg through the succession of refurbished rooms, bits of her napalmed psyche were strewn everywhere. Kitchen, bathroom, living room and all the upstairs bedrooms (especially the one that had been hers) – her whimpering, snarling, grieving presence haunted them all. She passed herself, sullen and vengeful, lurking on the stairs. Walked smack into herself sneaking about the landing, eavesdropping her parents' bitter fight. And splattered everywhere, on every floor, ceiling and wall, was the hurt and fear her father's cruel spite had blasted from her heart.

'When we moved here the bathroom was in a terrible state,' Mrs Greenberg told her, proudly indicating the gleaming avocado suite. 'We had to replace everything. And the shower was installed only months ago. I had a friend from New York staying recently and she claims it's as good as hers. Which is quite a compliment, seeing that American showers are known to be the best.'

Mrs Greenberg had a disturbingly unbalanced face. The top half was well arranged: nice, widely spaced blue eyes and small straight nose. The bottom half, however, seemed to belong to a much larger person altogether. The mouth – a cavernous orifice with alarming teeth – was set in a lantern jaw so loosely hinged it swayed like a suspension bridge in a wind. She looked like a marionette Kate was given as a child and whose head fell off the first time she played with it.

'I like the wallpaper.'

'Laura Ashley. I've got the same in the toilet.'

The toilet was their last port of call. As well as the Laura Ashley wallpaper, the toilet bowl now had a fitted lid cover and matching floor mat in a fluffy blue.

'I don't know about you, but I prefer a separate loo. It's so much more convenient.'

'Especially when you're enjoying a good, long soak.'

'Precisely,' said Mrs Greenberg, and they both laughed.

While they talked Kate eyed the door lock, wondering if it had been changed. Shortly before her mother upped and left, it jammed, trapping her inside (modesty obliged her to lock the door even when she was alone). A neighbour, alerted by her frantic cries from the window, called the fire brigade. Relieved and grateful though she was to be released, she told her daughter that being found by her strapping young liberators in a see-through nylon nightie was something that would always make her burn with shame.

As the tour progressed Mrs Greenberg became increasingly friendly. She was gratified by the intensity of Kate's interest, which extended to even the most insignificant details. Of all the prospective buyers she'd seen in the two months the house had been on the market, Kate was by far the most promising. So promising, in fact, that she did something she had not done before. She invited Kate back into the kitchen (still fitted with the same cream and brown units) for a cup of tea.

'The thing about this house is it's a happy house,' she confided, filling the electric kettle at the sink. 'And according to the previous owner it always has been. "Mrs Greenberg," she said to me the first time I came to look round, "I've had twenty-five joy-filled years here. My children are grown-up now, of course, but echoes of their carefree laughter fill every room."'

'Is that what she said?'

'Her very words. But I knew it without her telling me, because I'd felt the positive vibrations the moment I walked in.' Mrs Greenberg turned towards her, jaw wobbling earnestly. 'I'm sensitive to vibrations – are you?'

Fifteen minutes later Kate took her leave. She was not alone. A small army of Kates trotted out with her. Big, small, medium-sized, titless, sprouting and fully formed, they skipped, dragged, peacocked and sauntered in front, beside and behind her. They swarmed on to the bus with her, swarmed off it with her, and no sooner had she opened the door of the flat than they took possession. Pouting, whining, chattering and grizzling they milled around clamouring for her attention. Wherever she looked there she was, flopped on chairs, sofa, clattering around the kitchen and sprawled on the bed. A hundred and one versions in miniskirts, maxi-skirts, jeans and school uniform, all noisily jostling for space.

It was mayhem!
She couldn't move without tripping over herself.

The confusion was further increased by the arrival of Heather, Maria, Lidia, Father, Mother and farmer brother. Even Daniele put in a brief appearance. He was in the same mood as the day he had driven through heat and traffic to take her to the airport.

'Just look at yourself,' he growled, jabbing an accusing finger in her face. 'Look what England has done to you. You're a mess.'

She was a mess, of course, but Kate did not want to hear it from him. And anyway, despite the chaos, she knew her Pied-Piper instinct had been correct. These shrieking and unruly split-offs belonged to her, after all, and it was appropriate that they should all be together under one roof. That said, there was still the question of what to do with them. She put the problem to the troubled thirteen-year-old sniffing disconsolately on the sofa next to her.

'You've got to understand that what's done cannot be undone,' she said helplessly. 'All that hurt and loneliness and rejection. There's no going back to make it better.'

The girl glared and her eyes filled with angry tears.

'The point is, you don't like me either. You couldn't wait to leave me behind.'

There was no denying that this was true. She was brooding, awkward, self-conscious and bewildered – plus, she wore ridiculous lipstick (frosted beige) and had the silliest backcombed hair. Who but a masochist would hang around someone like that any longer than they had to?

'So what do you suggest?'

'We could try being friends' (now it was her turn to look Kate up and down). 'After all, you should be more understanding now you're middle-aged.'

'Now you're a wise old broiler,' Heather chortled.

'Now you're old enough to take responsibility for what you were, what you are and what you will be,' Lidia said.

This made sense. And, anyway, accepting herself was something Kate now felt ready for.

'OK girls,' she said, clapping her hands for order and attention. 'I suggest we have ourselves a Welcome Back party,' she grinned as her ears rang with an enthusiastic whooping, cheering response. 'So what are we waiting for? Let's put on the music and rock!'

Chapter 23

That night Kate took the striped sock out of the wellington boot, smoothed out the rolled-up notes and counted her stash. This took no more than thirty seconds, for there was only £145 left. Whatever the confusion of her heart and mind, the reality of her economic situation could not be clearer. She had to get a job. In truth, this moment of reckoning had been lurking ever since that momentous juncture when she knew she was never going back to her marriage (which occurred as, tear-streaked and unsteady, she disembarked from the Rome-London flight with the corpse of her aborted life stuffed messily into her hand luggage).

Kate was not a lazy woman and never had been. The only reason she had put off facing this reality was because the prospect of looking for work terrified her. After all, what could a redundant wife and mother like herself – unskilled, middle-aged and emotionally unstable to boot – possibly have to offer?

Answer: sausage sandwiches.

This revelation did not come about through any creative thinking of her own. It was presented to her by Sean after a fraught day trying to run his newly inherited business on his own. His clumsy bungling of the fry-up side had resulted in a string of dissatisfied customers, one of whom examined his burnt offering and refused to pay. This particular man sold phosphorescent plastic skulls a few yards from Phil's weekend pitch outside the antiques market at Camden Lock. 'Jesus, didn't your mum teach you anything!' he exclaimed, spitting out a mouthful and chucking the rest into the gutter. 'If you can't do better than this, mate, you'll be bankrupt before you know it!'

He was one of Phil's regulars, so Sean didn't attempt to argue. Besides which, he knew it was true. But he was so demoralized, so pissed off – so thoroughly and utterly – *gutted* – that even though it was only mid-afternoon he packed up and drove round to see Kate.

The reason he went to see Kate was because he wanted her comforting attention while he grizzled. He wanted her to envelop him with indulgent affection as she had when they first met. Most of all he wanted her to tell him not to worry, because there was nothing in the world she could not and would not make better. These fantasies were instantly dislodged, however, by the grim set of her mouth when she answered the door. And although she let him in and gave him a cup of (instant) coffee, her welcome was lukewarm. Less than lukewarm, in fact. It was positively chilly. For example, when Sean stretched out a hand to take one of her cigarettes, she snatched up the packet and told him sharply to buy his own.

But he tried anyway. Shoulders hunched, inky eyes heavy with self-pity, he cracked his knuckles and in a monotone whine proceeded to reel off the successive disasters of his unfortunate day. It was when he began describing the fat-sodden and charred food item which had broken his spirit that Kate got the message.

'Sausage sandwiches,' she said, interrupting. 'You want me to make the sausage sandwiches, don't you?'

'I'm desperate, Kate.'

'Aren't we all.'

'No, seriously. Will you help?'

'Well, that depends on what you're paying.'

Sean could hardly believe his ears. The Kate he knew and loved would have offered her services just to encourage and support. She was not sharp and upfront about money. He stared at her reproachfully but she returned his gaze unmoved.

'Well?'

'Twenty-five quid, cash in hand,' he said, sulkily. 'That's what Phil gave me. It's the standard rate.'

So the following day – which was Sunday – Kate took over the sausage sandwiches. And the bacon and fried egg jobs too. At two-foot square the kitchen space was smaller than anything she had ever experienced, but otherwise it was all pretty familiar. By the end of the day they had got through six large loaves of sliced white, two dozen eggs, thirty rashers of streaky and a similar quantity of pork sausages. And no one complained. Total takings were £157.50, and Sean was ecstatic. 'You and me are a winning team, Kate,' he crowed triumphantly as they closed up. 'We must stick together. No way we'll let greasy wops get us down.'

That was how it started and, for a while at least, that was how it went on. During the week they operated from Phil's second pitch in Rotherhithe and on Saturday they moved back to the Lock. Being his own boss – and pocketing all the profits – suited Sean down to the ground. Overnight he waved boyhood goodbye and embraced muscle-flexing, testosterone-driven, sex-obsessed manhood. He grew a beard, started calling Kate 'woman' (as in 'Get a move on there, woman') and flirted outrageously with every female customer between the ages of fourteen and sixty-five. He also talked about penis size so often it occurred to Kate he might have a problem.

'Heard this one? Why are women so bad at parking

cars? Because blokes are always telling them that six inches is twelve, that's why! Seriously though, it's said that the reason old Rod Stewart pulls the best-looking birds is that he's got a dong that hangs down to his knees. A real meat loaf, by all accounts. A guy I was at school with had a monster like that. Fully erect, it was ten inches long and three and a half inches thick – and I know that for a fact because a group of us measured it. Still, that's not really the point, is it? It's what you do with the bugger that counts.'

Yeah, yeah.

Sadie was much put out when she heard about the job. She had grown used to Kate always being available when she needed her. She suggested prostitution ('the sky's the limit if you know your stuff') as a more profitable and less time-consuming way of making money. Once reconciled to the fact, however, she incorporated it into her social routine. She arrived each Saturday afternoon around five and hung about eating fried-egg sandwiches until they closed at six. Then the three of them joined Nix and other stallholders who gathered in the 'traders' pub to swill beer and whinge about sales.

  Sadie liked market people. She liked their energy and their appetite for no-holds-barred fun. There was also the fact that she had started to think of getting an occupation herself and felt it was the right milieu for inspiration. The job idea was only partly influenced by Kate. It was mostly a response to the void created when she kicked Pete out of her life for ever. It happened the night after Nix's party. Bleary-eyed and still hung-over, she walked into the (carelessly unlocked) bathroom and discovered her lover indulging in a spot of vigorous self-abuse. Even then it wasn't so much the wanking she objected to as much as the magazine he was drooling over. Page after page of wanton anorexics, none of whom were out of their teens.

The real problem, of course, was that Sadie had never stopped grieving for the loss of her slim self. Furthermore, she refused to accept that it was the quantity and calorie content of the foodstuffs she gorged that caused her physical abundance. As far as she was concerned it was cosmic retribution. A mean-spirited, puritanical slap on the wrist for having been one of life's beauties and making the most of it. Nix, who had assumed the fight against puritanism as one of her many causes, was prepared to agree with the principle. 'But you're missing an important point,' she insisted during a conversation on the matter. 'As a businesswoman I can tell you there's a lucrative market for what you've got out there. Don't you agree, Kate?'

At that point Kate, tired and smelling a tad rancid from a day's frying, felt unable to contribute anything helpful to the debate. But later on, while waiting for the tube, she spotted a magazine lying face down on the platform and was gripped by a compulsion to pick it up. A quick, surreptitious flick revealed that it was entirely dedicated to the celebration of enormous women. Kate slipped it into her bag, marvelling at the workings of coincidence in Camden that night. Not only did she think it would boost Sadie's confidence, she was also convinced that *Bounteous Beauties*, as the publication was called, would relaunch Sadie's modelling career.

And when Sadie saw it, she was too.

Bounteous Beauties was the extravagant indulgence of Sir Reginald Marchant-Jones (affectionately known as Piglet for his squeaky voice and falsetto giggle). He started it because he could not find anything which presented seriously large ladies to his satisfaction. That is to say seductively, but also with good taste. He was fifty-two, a small whippet of a man with thinning blond hair and a pink face which turned an alarming puce when any of his emotions were aroused. The most notable thing about him, however, was the inherited fortune which allowed him to do just what he wanted at all times. This included dabbling in water-colours, going to the opera and taking lots of holidays. And worshipping female flesh at its most rippling and profuse.

B.B. was a new venture. The issue Kate picked up that Saturday night at Camden Town tube was only the third. The fourth was in the process of being prepared. Assisting Sir Reginald in this task were a photographer and a graphic designer, both established professionals who were involved because they too were devotees of fat. The very day that Kate happened upon the magazine the three men had spent the entire afternoon huddled over the light-box in Sir Reginald's study arguing about which model should grace the cover. Like philatelists looking for special markings, they compared the merits of folds, overlaps, mounds, hillocks and dimples. Eventually a decision was reached. It would be Marguerite, a formidable twenty-stone redhead who had been in every issue since the launch. This was immediately and unanimously revised, however, when a few days later Sadie's polaroids plopped through *B.B.*'s letter-box.

Taken by Pete in a moment of playful intimacy, they showed her stripped to her red satin camiknickers, posing languorously with a glass of champagne on her flouncy bed. Her pretty face swam above breasts the size of goose-down pillows. Her thighs rippled like snowdrifts. She looked so delectably creamy, so superabundantly luscious, that Sir Reginald was quite literally overcome.

'A star is born!' he gushed reverently, once he had

recovered and got her on the phone. 'You are the goddess I have spent my life looking for. You are everything *Bounteous Beauties* is about!'

Which was more or less what Sadie had spent the past fifteen years waiting to hear.

As well as highjacking the cover (for which Sadie wore the same camiknickers of Pete's polaroids), *B.B.* dedicated six pages to her, frolicking naked but for diaphanous drapes among trees and statuary in the wintry grounds of Sir Reginald's country estate. She caught a streaming head cold which kept her in bed for a few days but did nothing to dampen her enthusiasm for the adoration she was now receiving. Adoration which became a tidal wave when the December issue was sent out to it's two hundred and fifteen subscribers.

'It's unbelievable! The entire readership has written to say how absolutely divine I am,' Sadie swooned deliriously to Kate. 'Piglet says *Bounteous Beauties* will double its circulation because of me!'

Kate was delighted for her and only wished her own job gave her similar satisfaction. Sean had stopped calling her 'woman', for which she was grateful, but he was now calling her 'Mum'. (As in 'Easy on the marge, Mum, or we'll never make a profit!') He had also started dating Pauline, who worked for a skip-hire firm and seemed to find his born-again machismo very appealing. He told Kate that, despite demure appearances, she was a tigress in the sack and showed her the scratches on his back to prove it. Like all real men, love and lust now occupied all his off-duty hours. Kate only ever saw him at work.

She didn't see much of Sadie, either. Sir Reginald kept her busy with dinner parties, country weekends and similar social events. Kate assumed it was an affair but

Sadie denied it. 'I was prepared to give him the odd bonk in the interests of my career, but luckily he's incapable. I don't know the details, only that its connected with a gruesome riding accident.'

'Why the magazine then? I mean, what does he get out of it?'

'Well, Piglet says nature always compensates for any lack. I mean, feet can take over the function of hands, can't they? And if you lose your sight, the other senses become heightened. In Piglet's case his brain has taken over from his genitals. I suppose that means looking at pictures gives him cerebral orgasms. Sounds fun, don't you think?'

Kate did.

Kate missed Sadie now that she was not around. She still met Nix for a lager at the traders' pub after work on Saturdays, which was just about the sum total of her social life. Most evenings were spent watching television followed by a bedtime bath. Occasionally, if it wasn't raining, she went into the garden to smoke a cigarette and stare up at the lighted rectangles punched into the backs of the houses. Mad Max, whose after-dark activities took place elsewhere, never turned up.

But, although she was lonely, it was different from the sort of loneliness that had afflicted her before. That loneliness had sucked the marrow from her bones. It had made her feel like a lifeless asteroid adrift in the freezing tundra of starry space. It had pitched her into the vortex.

'You know something,' she said to Lidia, summoned from her cruise to attend Kate's thoughts. 'I'm really making progress. Things are not the same as they were a few months ago. At last I'm beginning to feel I belong to me.'

Lidia beamed. '*Brava figliola*. Not that I ever doubted

you for a moment, of course. But the question now is where do you go from here? In my opinion you need a long-term plan.'

Kate sighed. 'You mean I must look beyond the sausage sandwich?'

Lidia nodded. 'Precisely.'

Chapter 24

Kate, who always listened to what Lidia had to say, took the long-term plan idea to bed with her.

'What I need is a goal. An ideal scenario,' she said loudly, manoeuvring between the worst lumps in the mattress and switching out the light. 'An inspiring purpose I can ride with confidence and resolve into the future.'

She lay back, stared intensely into the darkness and focused on finding an answer. She knew it was there; its presence was tangible. Sooner or later it would reveal itself like a starburst of fireworks in a clear night sky. After half an hour nothing had happened. At which point she rolled up a mental sleeve, reached deep into the magician's hat and tried grabbing it by its twitching ears.

Niente!

So she switched on the light again, lit a cigarette and looked the problem square in the face. At which point it became obvious what the problem was. The reason she could not come up with a long-term plan was because her world was small and flat and not made for temporal adventuring. When her brain attempted to reach beyond the concept of the week after next, it simply got vertigo and fell off the edge.

The next day was Wednesday, Kate's day off. To ensure

the backlog of chores got done, she followed a rigid routine from which she never deviated. First came the housework. For several hours the flat was attacked with environmentally polluting substances (anionic surfactants, phosphates, chlorinated calcium hydroxide, and so on). After which she blitzed herself (deep skin-cleansing, leg-waxing, eyebrow-plucking, hard skin removal). She generally finished around three in the afternoon, after which she treated herself to a cappuccino at Luigi's.

When she awoke that morning, however, the long-term plan idea was the first thing that popped into her head. This was not a good sign.

'Oh, *no* – not another obsessive trip,' she groaned. 'If I don't take myself out today, I'll drive myself bonkers!'

So, abandoning normal procedure, she threw on her clothes and took herself off for breakfast at the café.

Kate had now been a regular at Luigi's for more than four months. During that time she had come to know the old lady who served food and presided over the Gaggia coffee-machine fairly well. Her name was Signora Caradonna, but in her mind Kate always referred to her by the English translation. Sometimes she called her Dear Mrs Dear-Woman. At other times Mrs Dear-Woman Dearest. And when she was feeling particularly affectionate, it was Dearest Mrs Dearest Dear-Woman.

She arrived to find Signora Caradonna (or Dear Mrs Dear-Woman as she was to Kate that morning) carefully wiping with a J-cloth the wax roses that stood by the till. Except for a lone man (reading a paper and flicking ash into the remains of a fry-up) the café was empty.

'*Buon giorno, cara.* How come so early?'

'I couldn't face the housework. I decided to have a change of routine.'

'That's good,' Dear Mrs Dear-Woman nodded approvingly. 'After all, a change is as good as a rest, they say. What you want? Egg, bacon and sausage?'

'Cappuccino. And one of those doughnuts, please.'

Kate carried her cup and doughnut to the table nearest to the counter and sat down. Spooning froth and nibbling the sugary bun, she watched as Dear Mrs Dear-Woman resumed tenderly administering to the flowers. Even here, however, the long-term plan idea – or rather the absence of a long-term plan idea – continued to plague her. She found herself wondering about Dear Mrs Dear-Woman. Had a long-term plan been the inspiration behind her decision to emigrate? And if so, was she satisfied with the way things had turned out? These questions continued to nag. In the end she could bear it no longer, so she asked.

Dear Mrs Dear-Woman put down the damp cloth. She leaned her elbows on the counter and smiled.

'I didn't have a long-term plan, *cara*. Except for bringing up a family, that is. But my Luigi did – he wanted to get rich. And he was so anxious to get started that we left Luzzi just two days after our wedding. Everyone begged him not to be so hasty, but the man couldn't wait to put the goats and the olive groves and the poverty behind him,' she sighed, shaking her head. 'It was the twenty third of April nineteen forty nine. I'll never forget that morning. Wood smoke rose from the houses like steam from cooking pots. The piazza with the church and the bar and the big, old tree was crowded with all our relatives. Everyone was weeping, even my sixteen-year-old brother, Cosimo, who took beatings from my father without shedding a tear. And you know something? If I close my eyes I can still hear the sound of the almond and cherry branches, loaded with blossom, clattering against the bus windows as we lurched and rattled down the steep, winding road to the railway station.'

Dear Mrs Dear-Woman fell silent. Her gaze slid effortlessly back to that determining moment in her distant past. And Kate's own gaze went with her. She saw Dear Mrs Dear-Woman dressed in her Paisley-patterned skirt and freshly laundered blouse, twisting in her seat to catch a last glimpse of her eagle's-nest village imprinted sharp as a paper cut-out against a cloudless blue sky. The nut-brown hair was shiny and neatly braided, the plump young face flushed. And every time she blinked, water splashed from her big, excited eyes.

This pleasant reverie was interrupted by a loud scraping as the man at the other table pushed back his chair, tucked his folded paper into his jacket pocket and walked out. Dear Mrs Dear-Woman picked up the J-cloth and resumed wiping.

'Luigi didn't get rich, of course, but he hasn't done badly,' she continued in a brisker tone. 'We've got a nice house with a little garden and despite the Chinese take-away and that Perfect Chicken opening two doors down, business is OK. Our daughters are married and we have five beautiful grandchildren,' she paused, glanced briefly towards the kitchen and lowered her tone. 'These are all good things and, believe me, I'm very grateful. But deep in my heart – how can I put it? – I've always felt something was missing. I suppose I've never quite found the happiness I was seeking.'

Ah, happiness! Top of everyone's agenda.
But what is it? Where is it? And how can one get some?

Had Kate put these questions to Sean when she arrived for work the next day his answers would have been: 1 – sex. 2 – bed. 3 – take Pauline's knickers off. She did not ask him, though, partly because she had little respect for his opinion, but also because he did not give her a chance.

Sons, Lovers, Etcetera

Almost before she had exchanged coat for apron he was into a monologue on vinyl versus CD. It went on for about thirty-five minutes and concluded with a declaration that – although he regarded his various Clash, U2 and Cure albums as boyhood mates – the sound-quality could not compare to CDs, so he was getting rid of the lot at a car-boot sale.

He seemed in a singularly hyped-up mood. His movements were twitchy and there was a lot of hair-raking and beard-tugging going on. This made Kate suspect he was merely warming up for something more important that he wanted to communicate. She was right. Pausing briefly to serve a customer with tea and a packet of crisps, he then revealed that at eight twenty-five precisely the previous evening, after the most spectacular bonk in the history of mankind, he and Pauline had decided to tie the knot. Furthermore, as they couldn't bear being parted for even the tiniest instant, Pauline would be leaving the skip company at the end of the week and starting work with him on the Monday.

Kate did not exactly jump for joy at the news of her imminent redundancy. What pissed her off most, however – aside from losing a hundred and fifty quid a week – was that Fate had been so impatient. Instead of giving her a chance to come up with a vision beyond the sausage sandwich, she was being shipwrecked before her hands had managed to grasp the helm.

'Sorry, Mum. But you do understand, don't you?'

'Understand what? That I'm vinyl and Pauline's a bloody CD?'

'Come on, you know how it is. Partners in love, partners in business, partners in life and all that?'

'Bugger off, Sean!'

And he did. With alacrity. Over to the Nag's Head for a

pint of Special Brew and half an hour on the fruit machines.

While he was gone a flailing drunk with urine-streaked trousers stationed himself a few feet from the van bellowing abuse at the rest of creation. The odium that streamed from his lips was like a choleraic evacuation from infected bowels. The only word in this poisonous mush that retained solid intelligibility was 'fuck' – or 'fugh' as he pronounced it.

And that, thought Kate, just about summed it up.

All in all, Kate had been employed for three weeks. She had earned a total of £450 and (by eating on the job and rationing herself to five cigarettes a day) had managed to save £280 of it. Added to the £145 she had started with, this meant there was now £425 in the kitty. Despite her talent for parsimony it was not a great sum – particularly with Christmas only two and a half weeks away. The proximity of this event stimulated a flurry of family phone calls. Lorenzo called to say that he was spending the festivities with his girlfriend in the exclusive mountain resort of Cortina, where her family had a house. Mother rang to warn that being alone at Christmas could make people suicidal and she should get in touch with her cousin Ruth in Pinner. Lidia rang to say that if she was homesick for Rome she could stay with her. Daniele rang to say they should dedicate the season of goodwill to marital reconciliation – somewhere 'warm and romantic like Tunisia'.

Kate did not relish the prospect of a solitary Christmas. She did not want to spend it in Rome with Lidia, however. Neither did she want to spend it in marital reconciliation. She certainly did not want to spend it in Pinner with Cousin Ruth, a woman she had never liked and had not seen for more than fifteen years. In fact, the only place she wanted to spend Christmas was somewhere lost to her for ever. And that was back down the years, when she still had sole possession of her darling boy-child and the whole tinselled caboodle shimmered with meaning. But Kate was not stupid, and she was perfectly aware that this attitude was pathetic and unhelpful. Which was why she became so exasperated when Heather, Maria and Lidia ganged up to nag her about it.

'For God's sake!' she snapped, hands on hips and nostrils flaring. 'A person doesn't have to be in therapy to know that unless they can let go, they'll never move forward!'

Exactly!

Having said this, however, Kate's thoughts on arriving at the street market with fifty pounds in her purse were all on Christmas past, not Christmas present. She was remembering the little red tricycle they bought Lorenzo the Christmas he was two – and the tantrum he threw when they refused to let him take it to bed. He also got a yellow plastic duck which survived as a bath time companion until the day he left home. Other notably successful Christmas presents were a Batman outfit when he was five, a Big Jim doll complete with changes of military uniform and firearm accessories when he was six, a Subbuteo football set when he was eight and an eighteen-gear Bianchi bike when he was twelve. At fourteen, having at last reached the legal age for a motor bike, Lorenzo got what he had spent the whole year campaigning for: a second-hand 50 cc Moto Morini. This, like the red tricycle, caused a tantrum. Kate – unconvinced by his declaration that he was an ace driver already – insisted he take proper lessons before she would allow him on the road.

Vida Adamoli

* * *

Back in the here and now it was a miserable day. A bitter East wind flapped canvas canopies and whipped discarded litter into an ankle-lashing frenzy. The Caucasian faces she passed were an ugly mottle of pink and purple, and everyone was in an impatient and irritated mood. For her part, Kate was not so much impatient and irritated as desperate. This was because she had set herself the task of finding the perfect gift for her son – and 'perfect' meant nothing less than the expression of her Immeasurable Love in tangible form. When he opened her package, she wanted the full force of her care and concern to leap out like a love arrow and pierce his heart.

Poor sod.

The market had a reputation for dodgy bargains. Which, having only fifty quid, was why Kate was there. But despite giving careful attention to polyester track suits, imitation leather wallets, trays of watches, china statuettes, pocket calculators, videos and so on, she came across nothing that looked dodgy in an interesting way. What she did find was a stall selling old banknotes, including a 1953 ten-shilling note. Lorenzo had started collecting in his teens and this was one specimen Kate knew he did not have. She congratulated herself on finding what she was sure would be a much appreciated stocking-filler.

By that time her hands were stiff with cold. At first she could not find her purse, and when she did it seemed to take ages of clumsy fumbling before she located the right change. The stallholder, a burly man wearing a knitted cap, watched her with pouched and malevolent eyes.

'Blimey,' he said with biting contempt when she finally found the coins to pay. 'That was like pulling teeth (teef), weren't it?'

Sons, Lovers, Etcetera

This hostile comment cut Kate to the quick. It was ridiculous, irrational – out of all proportion, if you like – but she felt that by perceiving her as niggardly while she was buying something for Lorenzo, he was judging her greatest love mean. Suddenly she lost her grip on a whole lot of emotion she'd been trying to contain. With hot tears pumping down her cheeks, she turned abruptly and walked off. She trod on toes, tripped over boxes, stumbled into pushchairs and ended up colliding with a tall black man wearing a stylish pair of suede desert boots. Despite her distress, Kate recognized him immediately. It was the karma-explaining minicab driver, Owen. Owen himself took longer to place her.

'No, no – don't tell me,' he insisted, snapping his fingers to jog his memory. 'I'll get it in a moment. It's not Jane. It's not Rita. It's not Karen . . . Hang on, I know! It's Kate!'

Chapter 25

Street Market. In the sheltering crook of Owen's arm.

Kate dug out a crumpled ball of hardened tissue that had been in her pocket for weeks and blew her nose. 'Sorry,' she blubbed.
'Don't worry about it.'
'No, really. This is awful.'
And it was – the tissue had become immediately saturated and it looked as if she would be forced to use her sleeve. Fortunately this humiliation was averted by Owen shoving a couple of man-strength jobs into her hand. Kate received them gratefully.
'Thanks,' she mumbled.
'My pleasure.'
Owen said this in the kindest and most compassionate of tones. Like the arm around her shoulders, his words drew her into a protective circle, a temporary oasis of comfort and shelter. Dissolving mascara was still streaming into her eyes and the turbulence was seriously affecting her vision. But the vortex, lurking a sly and slippery step away, could not have been clearer.
Damn the bugger!
They were standing conveniently near to the Blue Star café.
'Come along,' said Owen. And, without removing his arm, he guided her towards it and ushered her inside.

Five minutes later Kate was already on her second cup of tea. The rush of hot liquid had been instantly restoring and she gulped it so recklessly she now had a scalded tongue. Owen, his rangy body slumped with laid-back elegance in the chair opposite, observed her with friendly concern.

'Better?'

'Much.' The tears had dried up and she managed a smile. She preferred not to think of the mess she must look. 'Thanks for rescuing me.'

'I'm glad I was there,' he replied, taking a mental note of her emotional temperature. From his expression the diagnosis was 'still feverish but over the worst'. There was a short pause, then he said, 'Perhaps you'd find it helpful to talk?'

Kate, actually a proud and rather private woman, preferred listening to confidences and did not find it easy to open up. At that moment, however, she needed no coaxing. Indeed, she was so eager to explain herself that she dispensed with the usual preamble and went straight to the nub.

'It's like this,' she said, frowning earnestly. 'Once I lived in a world where things were solid and had meaning. I had a place and a function. I knew who I was and why I got up in the morning. But then life moved on and it all fell apart. Since then I've been trying to become someone I can identify with, someone I can recognize. I mean – and this is the real crux – where do I find my point of fixity in this world of change?'

'Good question,' said Owen. 'Put it this way. We all live on the edge of chaos. Our only point of fixity is to see life as precious and significant regardless of the ups and downs of our circumstances.' He closed his eyes and sat for a moment in silence. Reopening them, he leaned towards her and said, 'Listen to this . . .'

And, lowering his voice, he began reciting something very beautiful and very wise. But, try as she might, Kate could not take it in. Her ears had become enraptured. She was further distracted by the fact that as he talked, Owen's face became suffused with numinous light. It continued to spread until his entire being was enveloped in a nimbus of shimmering intensity. At which point he started levitating majestically towards the ceiling.

Now as we know, Kate was familiar with impromptu phenomena of the visionary kind. But even she found this spectacle pretty amazing.

'You're a philosopher!' she whispered reverently.

Owen shook his head modestly. 'No. An actor, actually.'

Which gave her the perfect cue to ask a few things about him. One of the things he told her was that, for the moment at least, he had given up minicabbing. He was back in work and in a play at a local pub theatre.

'That's brilliant.'

'Do you like the theatre?'

'I haven't been for years.'

'Come tonight then. I'll get you a complimentary ticket.'

Kate left Owen with a new sense of perspective. Quite what the new perspective was she could not say, but it enabled her to resume searching for Lorenzo's Christmas present in a brisker and more matter-of-fact state of mind. As a result she purchased a navy-blue cable-stitch sweater (Lorenzo looked very handsome in navy blue), which she posted off with the old ten-shilling note and a card showing Santa trying to squeeze his fat belly down a chimney. Inside she scrawled a big heart with a smiling face, dancing legs and a speech bubble which said: 'Happy Christmas, sweetest darling!'

It was surprising how easy things could be if you let them.

The show turned out to be a musical farce about a bungling Lothario who gets his comeuppance when he tangles with two smart and vengeful girls. As far as Kate was concerned Owen sang like Nat King Cole, danced like Fred Astaire and played his Lothario with more comic charm than Lenny Henry. In fact, she could not understand why he was not an international star. The audience had a great time, laughing at all the jokes and at the end of the performance giving it a stamping, whistling ovation.

Among those hanging around afterwards to offer members of the cast their personal congratulations was a burly man with a fierce nose and a head as bald as an egg. On catching sight of Kate (sitting a little self-consciously on her own), he fixed her with a probing stare. Then he broke off the conversation he was having with a bearded Rasta and hurried over.

'Well, what do you know!' he exclaimed, with a grin of surprised delight. 'Little old Kate! Remember me, Roy Steiner? We were at art school together.'

As it so happened she did. Which was surprising, given that the last time Kate had seen him he was in possession of a wild thatch of Dennis the Menace hair. Furthermore, just one single memory (neatly packaged in a Gertrude-type memory box) had survived the years: the occasion he invited her to dinner and prepared a Chilli con Carne that was all gristle. Traumatic though this was – she had never been able to face mince again – it was not the reason that this fragment of personal history had been logged for ever. No; that was caused by an acute attack of vaginal dryness. So acute, in fact, that when the food business was over and they turned to the real business of the evening, poor Roy had been unable to insert a finger, let alone anything else.

It was not disappointment at being deprived of the joys of penetration that had left the indelible mark – on that count Kate couldn't have cared less. It was the fact that her failure to lubricate exposed her squirming and panting as pure fake.

Which, for an aspiring sixteen-year-old sexpot, was mortifying, to say the least.

Roy – out of delicacy or genuine amnesia, who could tell? – gave no indication that this sensitive incident had lingered in his mind. His recollection was of a different occasion entirely, which Kate had totally erased. It was of an end-of-term party when she and another girl performed a reckless cancan and fell flat on their bums.

'A million years ago,' he said, shaking his polished dome and laughing.

A million years ago. The phrase stuck in Kate's mind and her thoughts buzzed around it all the way home. In her present world, for example, a million years ago was any of the grey time-frames that lined up shoulder to shoulder to form an average week. Their details, the incidents that marked their passing, sank as soon as they occurred, never to be raised again. Occasionally a remembered image might flare into random, inconsequential focus, only to flare out just as suddenly. Mad Max appearing over the garden wall, say. A face glimpsed in the street. Or wintry sunshine highlighting toast crumbs scattered sluttishly down her front. Even Louisa's dramatic visit to London was a million years ago now. Louisa, naked with Daniele in their marital bed, on the other hand, was eternally fixed in the here and now.

But it was Lorenzo, from first breath to young manhood, who was her most constant present. She was hooked up to every memory of him like a coma patient to an intravenous drip. She nourished herself with reminiscences. Grew drunkenly delirious with nostalgic longing. Glutted herself on what once was.

So why the hell should she give it up?
It was like sucking on nectar.

Back at home she ran a hot bath and soaked in a froth of Dewberry bubbles. Condensation streamed down the walls. Spumy water lapped at the floating islands of her knees, belly and gently bobbing breasts. Closing her eyes against the glare of the naked light-bulb, she reflected on chaos and fixity and identity and on learning to value her life.

'I understand what you're saying,' she told Owen, whose face even now hovered before her like a helium balloon. 'You're saying that this is a rite of passage. I must reset the compass. From this moment on, my first point of reference must be myself.'

And then she got it. An idea so exciting her eyes snapped open and she was propelled like a flying dolphin right out of the bath. She would consecrate her enlightened intention in the form of a mural painted on one of Heather's dingy bedroom walls. In reality, her creation would be much more complex than a simple mural. It would be nothing less than a figurative mandala symbolizing her heroic search to reunite herself.

'I see it now,' she said in a tremulous voice. 'In the centre there will be me, regal as a queen. I will be standing in the Garden of Infinite Value which, according to Owen, is the true reality of my existence.' She shook her head, awestruck. 'I'm brilliant,' she whispered. 'Bloody brilliant!'

And it was true – she was.

Sort of.

Chapter 26

The best painting Kate ever produced was of a reclining female nude, done in her final year at art school. The brush strokes were broad, the paint thick and the colours murky. It took her a whole three weeks to complete and it earned her the fulsome praise of her most revered teacher (whose style she had slavishly imitated). The model herself, however – a woman almost as fat as Sadie – was less complimentary.

'I hardly look human,' she complained, when she came to see the degree show exhibition. 'More like a pile of grubby pillows someone's dumped on the floor.'

At the time Kate dismissed her as a philistine who, unlike herself, knew nothing about Real Art. Furthermore – as she later sniggered to her friend, Stanley, who had overheard the comment – 'grubby pillows' was precisely what the model's graceless surges of slack, mottled flesh did look like. In later years (long after her mother gave the masterpiece to a charity jumble) the painting came to represent a moment of triumph, an indication of the important artist she would surely have become if things had turned out differently.

Her thoughts now returned to it in the context of her planned project, which her mind's eye saw as fresh and bright and vividly pictorial. This being so, it was clear that the mastery she once possessed (for denseness, laboured technique and overall oily sludge effect), and which might just have survived the years of neglect, would be useless to her now. The mural was a whole new vision and as such would require a whole new way of doing things.

Many aeons back Kate had come across a Goethe quotation that impressed her so much she learnt it by heart. It went: 'Concerning all acts of initiative there is one elementary truth, the ignorance of which kills countless ideas and splendid plans – that the moment one definitely commits oneself, then Providence moves too. All sorts of things occur to help one that would never have otherwise occurred.'

As most of her life had been spent as a person to whom things happened, rather than the other way round, she had never experienced the truth of this intelligence. But now, brimming with resolve and direction, Providence stepped in to help her in two very useful ways. First she found a book called *Learning to Draw* (squashed at the back of the airing cupboard of all unlikely places). This prompted a couple of days sketching oranges, her naked foot and the straggly spider plant that lived on the living-room mantel. Then she received a rush of Christmas presents in the form of cash donations, the generosity of which allowed her to invest a small fortune in brushes and acrylic paints. Her mother had sent one hundred and fifty pounds, Lidia fifty and Daniele – surprise, surprise – actually coughed up three hundred. Even Sadie turned up unexpectedly with an offering of several crisp, twenty-pound notes.

'Think of it as agent's commission, darling,' she insisted when Kate tried to protest. 'If it hadn't been for you I'd never have known about *Bounteous Beauties* or had the opportunity to meet Piglet and relaunch my modelling career.'

Sons, Lovers, Etcetera

True, of course, but nice of her just the same.

Work on the mural commenced on 15 December. As the bedroom was decorated with faded floral wallpaper, Kate was obliged first to paint the whole room white. It took three coats to cover the ghastly little sprigs and she was at it from eight in the morning to well past midnight. The next day she started a drawing of herself, naked and life-size, in the centre of the wall that was to be her canvas. She started with her breasts – which she portrayed in their glorious, pre-lactational perfection – and drew the rest of her body around them. If the result was rather pneumatic and top-heavy, it was also seductively pleasing. Or rather, it pleased Kate and that was what mattered.

Overall the pose was classical, with the right leg bent slightly and a generous curve to the left flank. In an attempt to convey both grace and resolution, she had one arm trailing lightly at her side, while the other was planted firmly on her hip. This theme was echoed in the dynamic contrast between the square definition of the shoulders and the gentler tilt of her head. As a final touch, she placed a garland of poppies (though she was equally tempted to make them cornflowers) around her head.

The following day she drew Lorenzo – or, rather, two Lorenzos. The first was Lorenzo *bambino* with angels wings, hovering up by the ceiling. (Never having drawn a baby before he looked more than a little like a huge flying worm). The second, placed a little behind her to the left, was Strapping Young Adonis, bare-chested and wearing jeans. (This was more successful as she copied it from a Wrangler's ad). Over the next few days other favourite people in her life made their appearance. Halfway up the wall was Maria strutting her stuff in red, tasselled knickers, black stockings and suspenders. Immediately below, Lidia radiated Glorious Widowhood from the comfort of a striped deck-chair. On the other side was a fourteen-year-old Heather wearing a regulation grey pleated skirt and pink frosted lipstick. A fourteen-year-old Kate similarly attired was squeezed in beside her. Last but not least came Mad Max, head high and tail erect, strolling past her feet.

The completed composition met with her approval. It had harmony and movement, with herself as the hub and her beloved ones spinning like the firmament around her. Now it was time for the painting and, once again, she started with the breasts. For these she chose a shade of the rosiest, most glowing pink, with a deep and vibrant coral for the prominently provocative nipples. When eventually she stepped back to assess her handiwork, Kate caught her breath. For there, leaping out at her with born-again fullness and buoyancy, were her lost treasures. The twin icons of her young womanhood. The jubilant mammaries which collapsed before they could conquer the world. And, in so doing, taught her the truth about permanence and impermanence. Hope and despair. Loneliness and grief.

For Kate, most things came back to breasts.
Sooner or later.

Things did not always go so smoothly, however. After all, what creative endeavour is without moments of struggle and doubt? Kate had a hard time with the clothes and perspective and, most of all, the likenesses. Indeed, Maria continued to resemble a Latin Carmen Miranda, while Lidia insisted on looking more like Dear Mrs Dear-Woman than she did herself. But she refused to be daunted. She was possessed of an awesome energy which grew with each successive brush stroke. The Indian proprietor noticed the change in her on the afternoon she bounced into the corner shop for milk and a packet of his best chocolate biscuits.

'Today you are a happy lady,' he commented approvingly. 'Could it be that Mr Right has turned up at last?'

He was a perceptive man and, as it so happened, not totally off the mark. The reason for the emergency dash was that Owen – as close to a Mr Right as it was possible to imagine – had paid her a surprise visit.

'I've just been for an audition for a telly play and I was passing your door,' he explained. 'It's not inconvenient, I hope?'

On each of their previous meetings Kate had been dazzled, stirred, moved and cerebrally excited. She had also taken note of his above-average physical attributes. Never before, however, had she felt the full force of his heart-stopping, drop-dead gorgeousness. That she did so now was largely due to the clothes he was wearing: brown suede jeans emphasizing the long legs and wonderful bum, black turtle-neck sweater showing off broad shoulders and well-honed torso. The other factor was the revitalizing effect her raised energy levels were having on her libido.

'Inconvenient? Goodness, no!' she reassured him, feeling as though her belly had suddenly spawned billions of wriggling tadpoles. 'I couldn't be more delighted. Really.'

Lust (as everyone knows) is thermally intense. For the entire duration of Owen's visit – just over an hour – Kate steamed with perspiration and her face was suffused with blood. Furthermore, every smile, every change of position, every time he curled his fingers around a biscuit and popped it into his outrageously sensual mouth, her colour rose. This – plus the fact that she was paint-splattered and had not combed her hair all day – conspired to make her more than usually self-conscious and awkward. Fortunately Owen's thoughts were still with the audition and he did not notice.

'Yeah, it went well. At least, I think it did. The casting director make a point of saying a few nice words to me afterwards. That was positive, at any rate. Mind you, you can never tell. So many times I've been convinced a part was mine only to see it go to someone else.'

'What part were you up for today?'

'Head of a space research programme. The play's set in a remote future when earth's dying and a search is on for a new planet to colonize. But every time a ship leaves the solar system it's attacked by mysterious forces and disintegrates. Then this oddball young scientist discovers that the universe is a giant organism and the mysterious force is nothing other than its immune system at work. The universe is inanimate and sterile, you see. It perceives life as a sort of cancer and instinctively moves in to stop it spreading.'

Kate thought it all sounded rather grim and said so.

'Well, that's science fiction for you,' Owen grinned in a way that made Kate's anarchic tadpoles even more frantic. 'I read loads of the stuff. I think it's great.'

As far as chocolate biscuits were concerned, Owen had an appetite rivalling Sean's. He devoured the entire packet. After which he kissed her lightly on the cheek, told her to take care and left. This brief contact pitched Kate into such confusion she was obliged to practise deep-breathing exercises before she could resume work. At which point she discovered that she couldn't get any of it in focus. Whichever part of the mural she looked at, all she could see was Owen.

'Well, what are you waiting for?' snapped Maria impatiently, who had announced her arrival by flopping heavily on the bed.

'Look, you've got a space up by the ceiling. There – opposite Lorenzo *bambino*. It's not very big, but at least you can fit his face in.'

And so she did.

The mural was finally completed at 9 p.m. on Christmas Eve. Kate celebrated with three slices of baked beans on toast and a whole bottle of Sainsbury's own-brand champagne. She consumed this feast sitting cross-legged on the floor in rapt contemplation of her curious creation. What was it, she asked herself? A mandala? The Owen-inspired Garden of Infinite Value of her original intention? And if not, what was the meaning of this Mardi Gras pageant of pink and yellow, red and green, blue and orange, violet and brown? Did it have any meaning, in fact? Or was it simply an expression of erotic fantasy? An undisciplined release of all her naïve and primitive impulses?

While pondering these questions the baked beans were eagerly ingested and the champagne thirstily downed. At the end of it she was replete, intoxicated, but not one jot the wiser.

All she knew was that she liked it.
It made her happy.
And in a strange and inexplicable way it made her feel free.

Chapter 27

Christmas day dawned grey and cold. It also dawned rather earlier than Kate had anticipated. Something had penetrated the woozy depths of her alcoholic repose and dragged her back to consciousness. With painful effort she unglued her eyes and blinked dumbly at the strange visitation standing by the bed. The figure was well formed and statuesque, wearing a silk shirt, thigh-length cashmere cardigan in creamy oatmeal, brown stretch-velvet leggings and unbelievably stylish, leopard-skin-print suede ankle boots. The hair fell to the shoulders in a sleek honeyed bob and the Rolex watch – well, it just had to be gold. Kate and the visitation stared at each other, then the hand with the Rolex reached out and rudely yanked the covers off.

'OK, donkey-breath,' it commanded. 'Move that fat ass of yours. Pronto!'

Despite the affected American drawl, it was the voice that identified her (because it had to be said she looked nothing like the teenage chum Kate had spent the past six months fraternizing with).

'Heather, what are you doing here?' she croaked disbelievingly.

'Get up,' was the terse reply. 'Then I'll tell you.'

So she got up, staggered zombie-like to the kitchen and stuck on a pot of coffee. While she did so Heather began yammering away, although Kate took in nothing until the coffee brewed and she got the caffeine fix that reactivated her brain. As a result she missed a whole chunk of the explanatory lead-in. Which, it turned out, was quite fortunate.

For Heather did not have a pretty story to tell.

'. . . I mean shit, man, you know me – the last thing I've ever been is a goddamn puritan. But that man was just too much. Every time I looked at his flaccid backside squeezed into the pretty panties he ponced around in I felt like puking. I'm telling you, it was seriously revolting. And it wasn't even that it got him horny. All he did was sprawl in front of the TV watching baseball and pulling his pubic hair through the lacy holes with a pair of tweezers. And even when he wasn't indulging his girlie underwear fetish he made me want to puke. I mean, the man's got a body like a goddamn ape. Long arms, short legs and hair all over his chest and back – get the picture? I'm telling you, Kate, it makes me *homicidal* to think of all I've put up with, just to discover he's been shagging the Mexican maid since the day we got back from our honeymoon. And under my very nose! Every time the filthy scumbag went scuttling to the kitchen she gave him a blow-job in the walk-in larder. Jesus, I was such an *innocent*! You know what I thought the day I found her shoving a raw courgette down her rattle-trap? I actually thought that was how she liked eating them. No way José. The bitch was practising her turbo-powered suction technique!'

At which point a phantom courgette the size of a prize marrow rose in her throat and choked her. 'Oh, bugger!' she wailed. 'Bugger, bugger, bugger and *bugger*!'

And then she covered her face with her hands and sobbed.

Sons, Lovers, Etcetera

By now it was still only 6.45 a.m. Kate's liver was still processing the effects of the previous evening's celebration. Her eyes felt as though someone had played marbles with them in a sandpit. Added to which, the collapse of Heather's brief marriage meant she would soon be homeless. All in all, it was remarkable that she felt as sympathetic as she did.

'I know how you feel. I've been there, remember?' she put an arm round the heaving shoulders and gave them an encouraging squeeze. 'But if a relationship's going to fail, then it's better it does so quickly. You know, before you've had time to get a whole new life in place. Believe me, things will work out, really they will. In no time at all you'll be settled back into your old routine. Everything will be just as it was before.'

At this Heather's head snapped up again. Her tears froze mid-flow.

'Oh, no!' she exclaimed, slapping her palm hard on the kitchen table. 'No, no and bloody *no*! My motherfucking husband is the hottest art dealer in New York. He puts Anselm Kiefers on the walls of the fucking glitterati. Our apartment on Central Park West has a fucking living room the size of a fucking bowling alley. Oh no, my sweets, there's no going back to how things were before! That fucking piece of dog-shit is going to give me a fucking divorce settlement that will see me fucking sorted for the rest of my fucking life! Get it?'

Kate smiled. She took their empty cups and refilled them with bitter black brew. From the sound of it Heather would not be wanting her flat back after all. Which immediately made her feel a whole lot better.

'That's the spirit,' she purred. 'You sock it to him.'

Stashed among Heather's six pieces of Louis Vuitton

luggage was a large bottle of duty-free bourbon, which she now produced. 'Just remember it's two in the morning as far as I'm concerned,' she informed Kate, cracking it open and prising the ice-cube tray from the furred-up ice compartment of the antiquated and juddering fridge. 'And as far as my body clock's concerned, two a.m. is party-time. In other words, sweetie, this is a perfectly acceptable hour to have a drink.' She poured herself a hefty bourbon on the rocks, then shivered into her cashmere. 'You know, I'd forgotten how primitive it is here. I mean, how did I ever survive without central heating?'

'Huddled over the gas fire?' suggested Kate.

'Yeah. Giving myself monster chilblains and red marbled legs. Come on, let's get comfortable.'

So they did. With cushions and cigarettes and the coffee pot and bottle of bourbon on the floor between them. And over the next couple of hours Heather elaborated further on her apelike, panty-wearing, filthy scumbag of a rich and cheating husband. For a start the man began life as a Lebanese carpet salesman. He had obtained US citizenship by marrying a wealthy widow when he was twenty-four and the bride a frisky sixty. Eighteen months later she failed to regain consciousness after a third face-lift operation and he was left everything. This background information was followed by details of his coke habit, his knuckle-cracking habit and his revolting nose-and toe-picking habit.

'If you ask me you're better off out of it,' Kate observed.

'That depends on how much I *get* out of it,' Heather replied vengefully, then her mind switched track and she giggled.

'Hey, remember that time we ambushed Mark Applewaite on his way back from football practice?'

'And told him he was driving us mad with lust and we wanted to have his babies?'

'Then we snatched his precious sports kit and he chased us all the way up the High Street to get it back.'

'And I was screaming "Rape! Murder! Get the police! The guy's a sex fiend and wants to ravish us!"'

They exchanged fond smiles, lit cigarettes and for a few silent moments were lost in nostalgic reverie. After which it was back to the crisis of Heather's present. By now Heather had told Kate everything, down to the number of times she'd had marital relations during the past month. Which meant the story had to be told all over again.

Help!

Heather had always been a woman who reinvented herself according to circumstances and whoever she was involved with at the time. Consequently, Kate was prepared for the fact that whenever they caught up with each other, she had to get to know her anew. This time, however, it was not her latest persona as rich-bitch wife of a New York big shot that Kate found it hard adjusting to. It was the contrast between her real-life presence and the younger and more malleable materialization she had become accustomed to. There was also the fact that Heather's incorporeal apparition disappeared the instant she was no longer relevant, while her flesh-and-blood counterpart did not. She was very much there, imposing her own agenda on the moment, and continued to do so until jet lag and bourbon finally overwhelmed her. Which, thankfully, just before eleven, it did.

'Happy Christmas, sweetie-pie,' she murmured sleepily. Then she stumbled into the bedroom and passed out.

This left Kate free to spend the rest of the day in semi-comatose recovery on the sofa. Except for visits to the toilet and occasionally switching TV channels, she did not stir until midnight struck and it was time to go to bed. Minutes after crawling in beside her friend, she was snoring. Three hours later Heather awoke, bright as a button and starving hungry. She went on a crashing, banging, clattering food-foraging operation that culminated in the preparation of *penne* with tuna and tomato sauce. Kate, subliminally irritated by the inappropriate nocturnal activity, responded by dragging both of the two pillows over her head. Lack of oxygen triggered a series of unpleasant dreams, the last of which featured Heather's husband sitting on her face and suffocating her. At seven she was rescued by Heather removing the pillow and barking 'Who did that?'

That, as Heather's jabbing finger made clear, was the mural. Kate was instantly alert, interpreting the fierce tone and aggressive body language as landlady outrage at belatedly discovering that her property had been vandalized.

'Me,' she ventured.

'You?'

'Me,' she repeated more boldly.

'I don't believe it.' Heather stared at her. 'I remember the stuff you did at art school. It was diabolical!'

'No, it wasn't.'

'It damn well was. But this, my sweets, is fantastic! I love it! It's wonderful!'

The words sang in Kate's ears sweeter than any dawn chorus.

'You really think so?'

'I really do.'

'Well, what can I say? I'm overwhelmed,' she grinned happily. 'Thanks.'

Back in front of the spluttering gas fire, dribbling coffee

and spraying toast crumbs, they substituted the subject of Art for that of Marital Breakdown. Kate's Art. Six months as an art dealer's wife had made an expert of Heather, as she was more than eager to demonstrate.

'In my opinion this new style of yours is sort of Naïve with a strong Pop Art influence. As I'm sure you know, Pop Art used lots of flat, bright colours to create a two-dimensional effect. Mind you, you can't really call the fat bird in stocking and suspenders two-dimensional, can you? I mean she's pretty pneumatic. In fact, she reminds me of one of those roly-poly females painted by Beryl what's-her-name. You know, that housewife from up North? Oh, you must have seen her stuff. She's rich and famous and her work's reproduced everywhere. Anyway, the name doesn't matter. The point I'm making is that she's a Naïve painter, too.'

'But what is a Naïve painter exactly?' Kate inquired, mostly to give Heather a further opportunity to hold forth. Heather seized it.

'To put it in a nutshell,' she said, dragging deeply on her cigarette and exhaling authoritatively through flared nostrils, 'a Naïve painter doesn't give a stuff about trends or movements or what anybody else is doing. He's got his own view of the world and he just gets on with it. And I don't know what you're looking at me like that for. I didn't totally waste my time with old scumbag, you know. I made sure I picked up a thing or two.'

One of the things Heather had picked up was the American accent. Another was the conviction that the world was stockpiled with idle money just waiting for Smart Guys to help themselves. And the first step to becoming a Smart Guy was to think like one. In the context of the mural, this meant assessing its commercial potential.

'For example,' she explained, 'I didn't just say to myself "I like it" and leave it at that. No, I immediately started thinking of all the people who would shell out to have a mural commemorating a significant moment in their lives. The concept I'm playing with here is nothing less than made-to-measure art. The client decides who they want in it and what they want to happen.'

Kate caught on immediately. 'It's a wonderful idea!' she squealed excitedly. 'I could do engagements and weddings and births and barmitzvahs and—'

'And divorces! Don't forget divorces!' Heather interjected, waving her cigarette wildly. 'In fact, sweetie, I'm going to be your very first client – once I've found a suitable place to live, of course. Can you guess the theme?'

'Screwing the bugger?'

'Exactly. And I want to be portrayed in a Katharine Hepburn-type suit, looking glamorous and triumphant with dollars fluttering like crisp autumn leaves all around me. On one side Arsehole hangs himself with his best pair of pink lacy panties. On the other Juanita chokes on the fistful of phallic vegetables she's trying to stuff down her gullet. In the background, Mother and Father stand arm-in-arm, gazing at me with love and pride.'

Kate listened enraptured. As Heather spoke she was mentally placing the figures in a surreal, Dali-esque piazza with stone balustrades, Romanesque arches and toppled bits of Corinthian column. The fact that she could not draw any of these things did not bother her (after all, she couldn't draw a Hepburn-type suit, either). The important thing was that she had discovered her vocation. Her creativity was rising like the moon behind

Sons, Lovers, Etcetera

the mountains. The sap in the trees. The song in the throat of the lark.
   Details like draughtsmanship and such would follow.

Sooner or later.

Chapter 28

For Kate marriage and motherhood were the things that had defined her. They pegged out her territory, provided the means for knowing who was who and what was what. It was a world under glass where lies, resentments and obsessive passions were nourished by stale and depleted air. In other words it was hell. But, as she pointed out to Heather, at the end of the day it was *her* hell, and to leave its confines had paralyzed her with fear.

Heather was touched by this confidence. Particularly since Kate had never been quite so frank with her before. Nevertheless, she was quick to assert that it did not reflect her own feelings at all. She was neither fearful nor paralysed. Quite the contrary, in fact. She felt wholesomely energized and was determined to capitalize on what had been the most profitable venture of her entire life. It was sad, she acknowledged, that her marriage had not conformed to the happy-ever-after scenario every bride hopes for. But she felt more than compensated by the improvement in her financial and social status (reflected in her undeniably spectacular wardrobe). As the estranged wife of a rich and successful man, she declared, she had moved from the cramped basement to the airy penthouse flat.

Which was one way of putting it.

* * *

This particular conversation was taking place in the bathroom. Heather – fortunately for both of them no longer jet-lagged – was enjoying a leisurely soak in the tub. She wore a green plastic bath cap and the gingery pubic hair Kate first encountered as dry tendrils stuck to the enamel now floated like a nappy island in the fragrant suds. Kate was sitting on the bath mat diligently attacking the hard skin on her feet with a corn knife. It was a very female situation; cosy, domestic and reassuringly chummy. Which meant, of course, it was inevitable that sooner or later the subject would turn to sex. And it did.

'Listen,' said Heather. 'Let's take a breather from marriage and inadequate exes, shall we? Tell me about your love life. And I mean present tense, sweetie, not past.'

Kate, at that moment intent on shaving a calloused ridge from the underside of her left little toe, glanced up briefly to pull a face.

'Oh, come on! I'm your oldest friend, remember? How many horizontal dates have you had in the last six months?'

'You really want to know?'

'I really want to know.'

'Zero.' (She had no intention of providing Heather with details of her vengeful copulation with Deiter.)

Heather was shocked. 'Zero! You must be climbing the wall!'

'Well, I'm not.'

'In that case, your libido's definitely atrophied. You know what they say, dear heart – if you don't use it you lose it.'

'My libido's fine,' retorted Kate, annoyed. 'And just the other day it swished its frisky tail to prove it.'

'Aha!' Heather's face lit up with a lascivious leer. She grabbed the sponge and began delightedly swabbing her freshly depilated armpits. 'So you've met someone you fancy. Who is he? What's his name? Has the bastard got a criminal record?'

Kate gave a loud, reluctant sigh. In truth, though, she was perfectly happy to be drawn on this one. And as she went on to describe his many and diverse attributes, Owen took shape before her. Indeed, so powerful was his imagined presence that she put down the corn knife, collected the shaved chips of horny skin in a piece of toilet paper and flushed them away. After all, it was not the sort of activity any self-respecting woman wants to be engaged in while her hero is around.

'Well I never!' Heather exclaimed, eyes fixed gleefully on her friend's half-turned face. 'You're actually blushing, you dirty cow.'

'I know, damn it!' admitted Kate.

Heather was in no hurry to renew contact with her premarital social set. It wasn't that she didn't like them, exactly. Just that they belonged to a world defined by career disappointments and Sundays with newspapers and a bottle of cheap wine in a lonely (and lumpy) bed. Kate's new acquaintances, uncontaminated by negative associations, sounded much more interesting. Particularly Owen, who she was certain had masses of equally interesting male friends. Meeting men was high on Heather's immediate agenda and she made no bones about it. Which was why she was so determined to convince Kate that they should throw a New Year's Eve party.

'But it's the twenty-eighth, for God's sake,' Kate wailed. 'How can we get it together in four days?'

'What's there to get together? We'll order the booze and get someone to cater.'

'It's not just a question of booze and food. A party needs

people and I could just about muster three. Besides which everyone will have made their arrangements by now.'

'You're so bloody negative,' Heather complained, seizing the nearest cushion and hurling it at her. 'Just pick up the phone and find out, will you?'

Kate caught the missile and tucked it comfortably under her bottom.

'Pick up the phone!'
'No.'
'Yes!'
'No, I tell you!'
And so it went on. And on.
Eventually, and just to shut her up, Kate gave in.

Sadie answered on the first ring. As her alternative was dinner with some of Piglet's more tedious friends, she was delighted to accept. As for Piglet himself, Sadie purred, he was happy with anything she decided. Next Kate tried Sean. He had set his heart on joining the revelries in Trafalgar Square, but Pauline stuck out for the party. Kate hung on while they argued about it, although the outcome was a foregone conclusion – anyone listening to that commanding tone knew that what Pauline wanted, Pauline got. She then phoned Roy, with whom she had exchanged numbers after Owen's play. He said he would love to come and looked forward to more reminiscing. He also mentioned he had four friends from Manchester staying with him, to which Kate replied, 'the more the merrier'. Owen, however – the point and purpose of it all – was out. Which meant she was obliged to leave a squeaky and self-conscious message on his answerphone.

Despite this setback, Heather was well pleased. She found the number of a girl called Shareen (who harked back to the period when she was thinking of opening a vegetarian café) who agreed, for a fee, to do the catering.

After which she trawled her address book looking for anybody it would not make her too depressed to see again. By lunch-time they had scrabbled together a guest list of seventeen – scrabbled being the operative word.

As Maria would have said, the party was meant to be.

Which left the booze. So off they went to the off-licence to place an order for red wine, white wine, *brut* vintage champagne, spirits and slimline tonic. Except for visits to the corner shop it was the first time they had ventured out since Heather's arrival. It was a cold, overcast day, rain lurking like a surly adolescent behind a low curtain of rolling cloud. The wind blew in sharp snatches, and when it did they pushed their faces forward and eagerly gulped the air. They needed it. The long lethargic hours huddled over the gas fire – not to mention all the duty-free bourbon – had given them fuddled brains and blood as thick and sluggish as pea soup.

They walked down the main road, past the library, hands thrust deep in their pockets, their strides synchronizing and picking up speed as they went. When they reached the cinema they doubled back and at the church turned off into streets of tall, flat-fronted houses with lighted windows chequering the winter gloom. As usual these bright rectangles drew Kate's eyes like magnets. They were living tableaux, boxed spaces of electric luminescence in which unique, never-to-be-repeated fragments of domestic intimacy were played out among the props of contemporary human existence; the chairs and tables, cookers and fridges, mirrors and potted plants.

Each fugitive life-moment, like a flicker on a TV screen, was caught by her probing gaze. A half-turned face, arms raised to pin back hair, a pot steaming on a stove, a newspaper picked up and opened. By witnessing them, she offered each ephemeral image a stay of execution. Through no will of her own these stolen pictures were transmitted by nerve cells and fibres to the memory vaults located deep in her cerebral hemispheres. And there they would stay, unacknowledged and undisturbed – except perhaps in dreams – until she snuffed it.

'Hey, look.' Heather breathed, nudging her in the ribs. 'Over there. Quick! Now that's what I call knicker-wettingly gorgeous.'

Kate turned her head. Across the street a young man stood framed in a first-floor window drinking from a can. He was stripped to the waist and the torso he so generously displayed to the world was lean, mean and seriously sculptured.

'Stop salivating, you old broiler,' she said impatiently. 'Groping a body like that's a thing of the past. And the time's come to face it.'

Heather was offended. 'Speak for yourself,' she snapped. 'A couple of months before my marriage I was having it off with a twenty-two-year-old aerobics instructor. I haven't told you about Chris yet, have I?'

And with that they were back to sex again.
But why not, after all?

What Heather missed most during her New York sojourn was fish and chips. Most specifically rock and chips, which she liked so doused in vinegar that the chips – fat-logged and soggy to start with – turned to mush. As this desire had remained long unsatisfied, they stopped at Larry's Fish Bar and purchased two steaming, paper-wrapped packages from which they contentedly stuffed their faces while dawdling home.

Approaching the off-licence again, still on the subject of Chris the aerobics instructor, Kate spotted Dear Mrs

Dear-Woman climbing aboard the number 19 bus. She was wearing a black coat, grey headscarf and a pair of pillar-box red high-heeled court shoes.

'That's Signora Caradonna,' she interrupted, taken aback. 'The lady from Luigi's café. What on earth's she doing in those shoes?'

'What's wrong with them?'

'They're risqué, that's what's wrong with them! And there's nothing risqué about Signora Caradonna. In fact, they're so out of character I almost thought she was someone else.'

'But how do you know what she's like when she's not working?' Heather asked. 'I mean, we are all someone else when our context changes. Aren't we?'

This was true of course. After all, since painting the mural Kate knew she too had changed her context (yet again), and as far as her future prospects were concerned, was now someone else. And yet the red shoes continued to disturb her. As she explained to Heather, it reminded her of finding condoms in her father's handkerchief drawer when she was twelve.

'I get it. Up until then you thought your parents had only done it twice, right? For the sole purpose of producing you and that horrible brother of yours?'

'Precisely.'

'Well, it's time to move on, girl. Take it from me, the fact that your Madonna icon wears red shoes is a reason for rejoicing.'

Kate laughed. Red shoes and rejoicing went well together and shifted her thoughts back to the party. Specifically the serious problem of what she was going to wear. Dropping her balled-up fish-and-chip paper into a bin, she slipped an arm round Heather's waist and gave it a squeeze.

'Look, you can say no if you want to, but . . .'

Vida Adamoli

'But . . . ?'
'About the party . . .'
'Well?'
'I was wondering if you could lend me something outrageously expensive and flattering to wear?'

Chapter 29

The dress Heather lent her was a Calvin Klein. It was silky, stretchy, clingy, strappy and, coincidentally, pillar-box red like Dearest Mrs Dear-Woman's shoes (she was still coming to terms with that one). On Heather it was a mid-thigh job; on Kate the hemline reached a couple of inches above the knee. The artful cut flattened her stomach, rounded her buttocks and restored to her breasts an almost juvenile buoyancy. Kate gazed with shining eyes at her reflection in the long wardrobe mirror.

'What do you think, then?'

Heather, still in her underwear, was absorbed in choosing between a classic black number and a draped affair in cream silk chiffon. 'Nice,' she muttered, a fag clamped between her as yet unpainted lips. Kate returned to the mirror unfazed by this less than rapturous response. She knew she looked gorgeous. So gorgeous, in fact, that she would have been perfectly happy to spend the duration of the party secluded in the bedroom admiring herself.

It was six-thirty on New Year's Eve. With the exception of Heather, everything was in readiness for the guests who would be arriving any time after eight. In the kitchen all available surfaces were occupied by the quiches, samosas, canapés, etcetera, that Shareen had delivered on covered trays earlier in the afternoon. White wine and champagne waited in the ice-filled bath, red wine and spirits on a side table in the sitting room. The shabby old sofa was fashionably draped in a white sheet, as was the equally shabby armchair. White hothouse lilies arranged in specially purchased white vases also contributed to the domestic face-lift. If they had not achieved *House Beautiful* exactly, it was certainly an improvement.

In the end Heather chose neither the classic black nor the draped cream. She opted for silver-grey harem pants with a backless halter top. She insisted Kate keep her company while she applied her make-up, which led Kate to suspect she was suffering from pre-party nerves. As it turned out all she wanted was to vent her pique that the 'oh-so-wonderful' Owen had never responded to the message Kate left. Kate, understandably sensitive about this, became hostile and defensive. The conversation was fast becoming spikier than Heather's quivering lashes (stiff with five coats of Max Factor's thickening and lengthening mascara) and might even have developed into a full-blown row when they were interrupted by the bell. It was Sadie, with a diminutive and pinkly adoring Piglet in tow.

'Well!' she squealed when Kate opened the door. 'Sex on legs! What *have* you been doing to yourself since I last saw you?'

Now that, thought Kate, was much more like it.

Sadie herself was blooming, if fatter than she had ever been. Or, at least, the black latex outfit designed especially for her by her now bosom friend, Nix, made her look so. This creation comprised an enormous bustier, hooked down the front, from which her breasts surged and billowed like giant rollers thundering towards the shore. Below this turbulence several miles of latex encased her belly and hips in a sort of mini. Heather – who like Kate had known her as a leggy nymphette at school and who emerged from the bathroom eager to renew their acquaintance – was rendered speechless by the transformation. Though not for long. When Heather's newly-separated status came up (immediately the effusive flurry of greetings was over) a spark was struck. They went to the subject of adulterous arseholes hammer and tongs and were to return to it with undiminished gusto on and off throughout the evening.

This left Kate to accompany Piglet to the bedroom to deposit their coats. She accepted the task as a routine part of a hostess's duty and certainly wasn't expecting gratification from it. This time, however, she was wrong. For when confronted with the mural, Piglet's reaction was even more enthusiastic than Heather's had been. Although perfectly honest about his partiality for the delicacy of the English water-colour (he rated Prince Charles's work highly), he confessed to finding Kate's garishly extravagant *opera d'arte* compellingly – indeed, almost alarmingly – alluring. This accolade, delivered in breathless, staccato bursts punctuated by the odd high-pitched giggle, soon had Kate as glowing and breathless as he was. It also made her garrulous. She launched into a long explanatory monologue, technical and other, which ended with them both examining the rippled detail of Maria's thighs.

Although the mural turned out to be the success of the party (Kate was delirious with delight at the way people kept wandering in and out to admire it), Piglet was the only one to put his money where his mouth was. And very generously too. He offered her a three-thousand-pound commission to put murals (featuring Sadie, of course) on three walls of the bedroom of his London house.

'What do you say?'

'Absolutely,' Kate replied, tripping over her tongue in her eagerness to accept. 'I'd love to.'

The fact that Piglet wanted to wake up cling-filmed in Sadie was no surprise. But that it should provide her with a career break was.

She had entered the room an amateur and was leaving it a professional.

Wow!

By nine-thirty most of the guests had arrived. Outside the temperature had plummeted to near-freezing. Inside it was rapidly steaming up as body heat supplemented the best efforts of the gas fire. Heather's disappointment at Owen's absence – or, more accurately, the absence of the interesting male friends she had convinced herself he would produce – was mitigated by the presence of Roy and his four Mancunian house guests. Indeed, these flirtatiously laddish beer-drinkers – who brought their own supply of Special Brew – raised the spirits of all Heather's friends (who, as it happened, made up most of the single women in the place).

Heather had Velcroed herself to Roy, whom she clearly fancied. Her long body swayed, arched, tensed and wriggled, beckoning him with a sensuous subtext as she held forth about New York and the glamorous and exciting life she lived there.

'I've only been back a week but I'm missing all that raw, sexy energy already,' Kate overheard her saying, in a voice that poured honey over gravel. 'But you know the place, Roy, so I don't have to tell you. You know what I mean.'

The reason Kate was half-listening to this conversation

was because she was bored by her own. Ruth, a woman Heather knew only slightly (which was why she invited her), was describing the nightmare of living with builders: the unreliability, the shoddy workmanship, the mess. It was the mess that caused her the most distress and she went on and on about it.

'To give you another example,' she said to Kate, her small freckled face taut with the remembered anguish. 'I made sure all the furniture was properly protected with heavy-duty dust sheets, yet I found a dirty great handprint smack in the middle of my cream sofa. Now you tell me – how did that get there?'

Kate shook her head with an expression that implied sympathetic bewilderment. Sean, however, who had once done a stint of painting and decorating, had no doubts.

'Listen,' he said. 'I can tell you from experience that house-proud women are the worst part of any job. They make your life a bloody misery. Take it from me, one of the blokes did it to avenge himself for all the nagging.'

Sean had rowed with Pauline on the way over and was not in the best of moods. Furthermore, he was still rankled by his Christmas card from Phil, which was unacceptably breezy and contained no solicitous inquiries after his welfare. He complained about it in terms that made Kate suspect his mother's lesbian defection – coupled with his own engagement and responsibilities as a self-employed businessman – was nudging him over to the moral right.

'I've made up my mind,' he told her when Ruth, offended by the suggestion that she nagged, wandered off and left them alone. 'The day Pauline gets pregnant I'm bringing a bloke in. To quote that German religious chap, Martin Luther, women should remain at home, sit still, keep house and bear and bring up children. Well, I bloody agree with him.'

He would have said more on the subject but at that moment Pauline summoned him from across the room. Kate observed the sullen set of his shoulders as he wove through the crush towards her and smiled at how quickly a kiss, a ruffle of the hair and a large slice of pizza relaxed them.

'Putty in her hands,' was the phrase that sprang to mind.

At Heather's insistence the evening started off with one of the Philip Glass tapes she'd brought back from New York. This was soon replaced by a reissued Motown compilation, however, and now people were jigging about to 'Jumping Jack Flash' with good old Jagger. Kate was just about to launch into a foot-stamping, hip-gyrating solo when suddenly someone crept up behind her and covered her eyes. It was a touch she immediately recognized. A heart-stopping touch that connected with her very soul. With a shriek of joy she seized the hands and spun round. And there he was, her son: tall, handsome and grinning from ear to ear. He was also wearing the navy-blue, cable-stitch sweater she'd sent him for Christmas. Just to please her.

For Carina, Lorenzo's girlfriend, maternal excess was part of her culture and something she also endured (although she was luckier than Lorenzo in having two sisters and a brother which helped spread the heat). She was well prepared, therefore – expected, even – the scene that followed, and looked on with indulgent composure. Not that Kate would have noticed had it been otherwise. For in that moment the room fell away, the people disappeared and the music magically silenced. She had her boy-child back. And nothing existed outside that.

'Why didn't you ring, darling?' she babbled, happy tears spilling from her eyes like festival fountains and ruining her make-up. 'I'd have met you at the airport. I'd have cooked something special. I'd have warmed your pyjamas and had your bed waiting!'

Lorenzo laughed, immediately lapsing into muddled Italish.

'*Dai, mamma.* Don't make the usual *casino*. I wanted to do a *sorpresa*. You're pleased, no?'

Pleased! She was so pleased she wanted to pick her cub up by his furry little scruff and secrete him away to a hidden lair. Things being as they were, though, she had to make do with the only privacy available, which was the bathroom. There her thrilled hands stroked and smoothed and plucked and hugged, as she plied him with a million eager questions. Which he dutifully answered, while doing his best to fend off the continuous assault of hungry pawings. But they both knew this was the way things were and always would be. He was her sun and moon, the jewel in her mountain, the spirit in her lake. Her love was like the harvest moon, and his beloved face the water that caught its rays.

Which was tough, of course, but Lorenzo could handle it. He had to, after all.

Half an hour later they re-emerged. The party sprang back into focus and Carina stepped forward to reclaim her prize. Kate, her emotions still in heated disarray, accepted a cigarette from Pauline and cast a distracted eye around the room. All seemed to be going well. People were either dancing, snogging or shrieking with hilarious laughter. With the exception of Sadie – inebriated and by now sweating profusely in her latex body armour – who was happily looting what was left of the food. Then someone switched on the television and everyone's attention was focused as the countdown to midnight began. And when it hit the hour, a great whooping cheer went up. Champagne corks popped, glasses were slopped full to the brim and lips made enthusiastic contact left, right and centre.

Kate craned anxiously to locate Lorenzo among the roomful of celebrating bodies. But, before she could elbow her way through to find him, she was seized from behind. This time she did not recognize the touch, although when she turned round she realized she should have done. For the place that she found herself in was one she had been in before: the sheltering crook of Owen's arms.

'You've come!' she exclaimed, her heart taking its second vertiginous leap of the evening. 'I'd given up hope. I mean, I thought you couldn't make it.'

'I spent Christmas in Trinidad with my folks. I only got back a couple of hours ago.' His arms hugged her closer.

'Happy New Year, Kate,' he said.

Then he kissed her.

And we're talking proper kisses here.
Long, deep and meaningfully breathless!

It was an eternal moment that ended with Owen's lips sliding from her mouth to her quivering ear.

'Is there any chance I can entice you away from here?' he whispered. 'I very much want to take you home with me.'

Now this really laid things on the line. Her sweet child for whom she would willingly sacrifice her life had only just arrived. Furthermore, the precious creature would only be staying for one short week. In such circumstances it was surely inconceivable that she would even think of absenting herself from him? Or was it?

Obviously not.

Sons, Lovers, Etcetera

'Let's go now,' she heard herself saying tremulously. And shocked, amazed and dizzily delighted with herself, she let him take her hand and lead her away.

Chapter 30

January 1. The slumbering hour just before dawn.

Propped up on one elbow, Kate gazed at Owen's naked body sprawled in sleep beside her. In the density of the dark his blackness lost its contours, becoming like the shadowy, unfamiliar shapes pressing in all around her. She brought her face closer, absorbing the sharp-edged sweetness given off by his skin. His odour filled her nostrils and she was rocked again with lust and wonder. And with each seeking breath she took, the silent room breathed with her.

Extricating herself from the tangled sheets, she slipped from the bed and went noiselessly into the living room. A dim glow from the street light below the window cast a yellow mantle over simple furnishings and the cups from which they had drunk coffee just hours before. She picked one up, and turned it in her hands. It was an object of significance, for it marked the last moment of their separateness. The moment before she took Owen into herself and understood that she was no longer adrift, but a woman whole and feeling and still capable of love.

These thoughts of love brought thoughts of Lorenzo, huddled on Heather's narrow and uncomfortable sofa with Carina. She recalled his outraged disbelief at her call to say that she was sleeping out but would see him the following day; the censorious click as the phone was banged down.

'There's no need to feel guilty,' Maria, almost invisible in the half-light, chided softly. 'You have a right to a life too, you know.'

'But I don't feel guilty,' Kate whispered. 'At last I feel free.'

Though barely audible, these words roared in her ears. Their deafening echo summoned a great white stallion with tossing mane and wild eyes that arrived with a thundering of hooves and whinnied to a halt beside her. And before she knew it she was up on its broad back, hair streaming, bare legs clamped round the magnificent flanks, galloping across a wide open plain with clouds streaming, wind whistling and blue hills beckoning in the distance.

And with that what more can one say?

Except to add that apart from the odd crisis, emotional freak-out, nostalgic wallowing and plain run-of-the-mill stagnation, Kate lived happily ever after.

Olé!